PRAISE FOR MEL

Diary of a Teen

It's My Life by C

"Melody Carlson creates a cast of characters who are real and engaging. It made me want to read the first book in the series, and hope that there will be more!"

NANCY RUE, BESTSELLING AUTHOR OF *Here's Lily!* AND *Lily the Rebel*

"Melody has done it again! Teens won't be able to resist Caitlin's latest diary. Teens will identify and laugh with Caitlin, and gain spiritual insight from this fresh glimpse into the heart of a very real teenage girl."

HEATHER KOPP, AUTHOR OF *LOVE STORIES GOD TOLD*
AND *I STOLE GOD FROM GOODY TWO-SHOES*

Diary of a Teenage Girl Book 1:

Becoming Me by Caitlin O'Conner

"As I read through *Diary of a Teenage Girl*, I had to keep reminding myself that I wasn't reading my own diary! It captures the thoughts and issues of a teenager's struggles to follow God's pathway."

RACHAEL LAMPA, TEEN RECORDING ARTIST

"From the first page, *Diary* captured me. I couldn't stop reading! This is a brilliant, well-crafted imaginary journey to the heart of a sixteen-year-old. I can't wait for the sequel!"

ROBIN JONES GUNN, BESTSELLING AUTHOR OF THE GLENBROOKE SERIES,
THE CHRISTY MILLER SERIES, AND THE SIERRA JENSEN SERIES

"As I read *Diary*…I felt as if I had been given a gift—a 'backstage pass' into the life and heart of Caitlin O'Conner. It is a wonderful and mysterious ride as we are allowed a rare chance to travel alongside a teenage girl as she lives in the real world. This is a unique and refreshing read—fun and entertaining, while at the same time moving and insightful. Read and learn."

GEOFF MOORE, CONTEMPORARY CHRISTIAN RECORDING ARTIST

"Creative and impactful! *Diary* drew me in as my concern for Caitlin and her friends grew stronger each page I turned. It gave me the inside story to issues I see in my own life—and among my friends and peers. I recommend this book to every teenage girl going through the struggles of peer pressure, dating, and other temptations we face in life."

DANAE JACOBSON, AUTHOR OF *THINGS I'VE LEARNED LATELY*

"Melody Carlson writes with the clear, crisp voice of today's adolescent. *Diary of a Teenage Girl* is sure to please any teenager who is struggling with peer pressure, identity, and a desire to know and understand God's will. A moving, tender story that will be remembered…and loved."

ANGELA ELWELL HUNT, BESTSELLING AUTHOR OF *THE NOTE*
AND *MY LIFE AS A MIDDLE SCHOOL MOM*

"Melody Carlson captures the voice of teens today in a character we can all relate to. The unique peer perspective makes it very effective. Integrating the crucial message of the gospel, it forces us to weigh issues and causes us to look at a young person—in reality, ourselves—objectively. It challenges, convicts, and leaves us with hope for the future. I highly recommend this book."

ANGELA ALCORN, CO-AUTHOR OF *THE ISHBANE CONSPIRACY*

"Carlson succeeds in weaving Christian beliefs into the plot with a light hand—and it's a darn good read!"

NAPRA REVIEW SERVICE

DIARY OF A TEENAGE GIRL

BOOK № 4

ON MY OWN

by Caitlin O'Conner

A NOVEL

MELODY CARLSON

Multnomah®Publishers *Sisters, Oregon*

ON MY OWN
published by Multnomah Publishers, Inc.,
and in association with the literary agency of Sara A. Fortenberry

© 2002 by Melody Carlson

International Standard Book Number: 1-59052-017-3

Cover design by David Carlson Design
Cover image by David Bailey Photography

Scripture quotations are from:
The Holy Bible, New International Version © 1973, 1984 by International Bible Society, used by permission of Zondervan Publishing House

Multnomah is a trademark of Multnomah Publishers, Inc.,
and is registered in the U.S. Patent and Trademark Office.
The colophon is a trademark of Multnomah Publishers, Inc.

Printed in the United States of America

For information:
MULTNOMAH PUBLISHERS, INC.
POST OFFICE BOX 1720
SISTERS, OREGON 97759

Library of Congress Cataloging-in-Publication Data
Carlson, Melody.
    On my own, by Caitlin O'Conner / by Melody Carlson.
        p. cm. -- (Diary of a teenage girl ; Book 4)
Summary: In her first year at college, Caitlin's diary reflects her homesickness, the challenges of rooming with a non-Christian, and evolving friendships, old and new.
    ISBN 1-59052-017-3 (pbk.)
    [1. Christian life--Fiction. 2. Universities and colleges--Fiction. 3. Interpersonal relations--Fiction. 4. Conduct of life--Fiction. 5. Diaries--Fiction.]
I. Title.
PZ7.C216637 Oq 2002
[Fic]--dc21   2002002723

02 03 04 05 06 07 08—10 9 8 7 6 5 4 3 2 1 0

OTHER BOOKS BY MELODY CARLSON:
Piercing Proverbs

DIARY OF A TEENAGE GIRL SERIES
Becoming Me
It's My Life
Who I Am
On My Own
My Name Is Chloe (February 2003)

ONE

Tuesday, September 3 (Independence Day)

It's what I've been wanting for ages—that irresistible reward that parents hold in front of their kids just like the old proverbial carrot—that tantalizing treat that only comes with "time and age and experience." Okay, I'm talking about <u>independence</u>! Today's my official "Independence Day," and let me tell you, it feels totally great! All right, Caitlin, let's settle down, girl.

Of course, I had hoped to sound much more mature when I started journaling in my first college diary (or maybe I should call it a journal now). After all, I might be an aspiring writer, journalist, or who knows what? But honestly, I did want my first college entry to sound—well, more grown-up.

On the other hand, a girl needs some place where she can just relax and be herself—let her hair down, so to speak. Especially when I've been acting so grown-up and mature for my parents lately, assuring them that I'm really ready for this, that I'll be okay, and not to be so concerned—you know the kind of stuff we tell our parents to get them to chill a little. But the bottom line is, I really do believe God is watching over me, so what's there to worry about?

And then, today—the big move in. I had to keep reassuring my dad that I was perfectly fine with this new transition. I thought I had him pretty convinced too, until it was time for him to leave. Then, with a stricken look on his face, the next thing I know he's double-checking the dead bolt on my door and making sure the phone is working. Sheesh, he even tested the smoke detector and then actually grilled me about which was the quickest fire escape route, which fortunately I had noticed on about our fourth trip carrying my stuff up the stairs. (It's at the end of the hall to the right.)

"Don't worry so much, Dad," I told him. "Hey, I even saw a fire extinguisher a couple doors down, and I'll bet it works just fine." I made a real effort not to laugh at what I know he feels is fairly serious business.

Finally we had all my boxes and bags and stuff stacked in my room, piled high and strewn all over the place like a tornado had blown in. (Dad believes that haste makes waste...) Thankfully my roommate isn't here yet, so I might actually finish getting the last of my things put away before she arrives. I hadn't realized I'd brought so much STUFF. In fact, I thought I was being somewhat of a minimalist. That is, until I saw all that crud heaped all over the room. As I suspected, Mom had thrown in a few extra items like an emergency food supply box, a first-aid kit, and even a mini medicine chest complete with Pepto-Bismol among other things! I guess she still doesn't think I can take care of myself, or maybe she thinks that I'm going to get ulcers here on my own. But I have to admit, it was sweet. And now that most of my stuff is stowed away, it doesn't look half bad around here.

Anyway, when it was time to go, my dad gave me this nice long hug, and then said all those typically parental things like: "We really believe in you, Catie. We know you're going to do just great." Nice stuff like that. And I'll admit I cried, although I tried not to show it since I didn't want Dad to feel any worse than necessary. I cried a little more after he drove away. But as I walked back toward the dorm, it hit me. I felt this wonderful rush, this new excitement, almost like adrenaline pumping right through me. I'm free! Independent! On my own! It felt so totally cool to realize this. It still does.

My mom had wanted me to join a sorority—her old one to be specific. And despite my concern that it might not be a very Christian atmosphere, I actually looked into it (mostly to please Mom). Then I was informed that they had a mile-long waiting list. Still, I could've gotten on the list if I'd really wanted and if I was willing to go through rush week. Which I was NOT. I really don't care for the idea of herding a bunch of girls around and trying to pick out the best among them. And the truth is, I think

sororities are kind of shallow and superficial.
Consequently, I liked the idea of a dorm better—plus it
seemed more independent.

I'm sure I could be wrong about these things, but
that's the general impression I got when I checked out
my mom's old stomping grounds. I know my good buddy Josh
belonged to a fraternity when he was here last year,
and he thought it was great. But then it was a Christian
organization. He'd even encouraged me to look into a
Christian sorority he knew about, but I figured if I wasn't
going to join my mom's, I probably shouldn't try to join
another. I mean, her feelings were already slightly hurt
when I told her I wasn't interested. No need to rub it in.
So here I am.

I already know my roommate's name is Elizabeth
Banks and that she's a sophomore (since it says so on our
door). But that's about all I know. I could have
requested a specific roommate if I'd known anyone coming to the university, which unfortunately I didn't.
Andrea LeMarsh thought she was going to come here,
and we'd talked about rooming together, but then she
found out her dad had lost everything in the stock
market last spring. And even though her tightwad step-
dad has plenty of dough, he wouldn't spring for tuition
plus room and board, so she decided to live at home and
go to community college for a year. And, of course,
Beanie and Jenny and Anna are all on their way to the
Christian college even as I write. But here's the kicker:
After all Mrs. Lambert put Jenny through last year, she

actually let her take a car. I couldn't believe it—that woman has really been changing lately!

Speaking of cars, my parents and I decided it was best to sell mine. I must admit to feeling a little blue at first, but I know it was the smart thing to do. There's no way I could work to make payments plus car insurance and go to school full time. Besides, everything's within walking distance here, and Dad even talked me into bringing my bike, just in case. But I still miss that little car—my first car. And it was a good car too. It took Jenny and Beanie and me (the three amigas) all the way to Mexico and back! Now I have to finish unpacking, just in case the mysterious Elizabeth should arrive tonight and trip over my shoes still piled on the floor.

Wednesday, September 4

So far no roommate. But that's okay with me. It gives me a chance to sort of catch my breath and get my bearings. I'm completely unpacked now, feeling almost at home with my familiar bedding and pillows and whatnot all around. I hope Elizabeth doesn't mind that I took the side of the room that's away from the door. I didn't really do it on purpose. I've just always had my bed on the right and automatically took that side. Hopefully she won't care. And if she does, I'll offer to switch. Although that means moving everything and taking down my bulletin board and posters, which took me forever to arrange just right. Before Dad and I left town, Beanie

Jacobs stopped by to say good-bye and to give me this cool poster with the Lord's Prayer on it. I hung it right where I can see it from my bed.

"God bless you, Caitlin," Beanie said as she hugged me tightly. I could tell she was crying, which was making me cry too. "I can't believe we're going to be so far apart."

"We'll e-mail," I promised, suddenly feeling the gulf that would soon separate us. "We won't lose touch."

"Right." She stepped back and wiped her nose. "And Jenny says that if we miss you too badly, we'll just hop in her car and drive on over."

I forced a laugh. "That's about three hundred miles, Beanie."

"Jenny drives fast."

"Well, tell her to take it easy." Then I waved to Beanie as I climbed into Dad's SUV, wishing I'd said something more meaningful, something profound and memorable. But I suppose that's kind of silly. I mean, it's not like I'm never going to see her again. In fact, I think I'll e-mail her tonight and see how their trip went.

I got an e-mail from Josh yesterday. He wrote to me as if he were personally welcoming me to the university (like he was still here). He invited me to attend his fellowship group, told me the best place to get coffee, reminded me not to be late to registration (which is tomorrow, by the way), and then warned me that dorm food usually stinks. I e-mailed back assuring him that I'm fitting into things just fine, thank you very much. Not that I didn't want his advice, but it did come across as a little overbearing. And this is something we specifically discussed several times this summer.

You see, as much as I like Josh, he sometimes has this annoying habit of coming across as—hmmm, how do I say this nicely—acting slightly superior or perhaps even chauvinistic. Okay, maybe those aren't exactly the right words. I'm not even sure how to describe it. But sometimes I almost feel as if he's telling me what to do or how to think. And I really don't appreciate it.

Now it's not that I don't respect or appreciate his wisdom, but it's more that I don't care for how he dishes it out sometimes. Of course, I never put it to him in quite those words. But that's kind of how I felt, and for the sake of our friendship, I did try to communicate it to him. And I must give him this: He does listen. And he says he wants to change. I just think it's an old habit or something. His little sister Chloe said he's always been like that. She calls it "just plain pigheaded," but I think that's a bit strong. Still, I'm glad I can be honest with him and he doesn't get mad.

I guess that's one of the things I like about our friendship—I feel free to tell him things that bother me, and he doesn't take offense. And I think our friendship really grew this summer. Although to be honest, it made me a little uneasy to have him around so much. He was working in town, and as a result, it seemed as if we spent a fair amount of spare time together. Now, despite Jenny and Beanie's teasing, it wasn't a dating situation. Not really. I mean, both Josh and I had agreed from the get-go that we were not dating or romantically involved. And to prove our point, we almost always had either my little brother Ben or Chloe or one or more of our other friends with us when we went anywhere. I know it sounds silly, but I also know it was for the best. And since this is a diary—and a secret place—I will say why I know this to be true.

You see, early in the summer, shortly after graduation, Josh stopped by our house one afternoon and just sort of hung out. He and Ben and I shot baskets for a while until it got too hot; then Ben went inside to get ready for a baseball game, and Josh and I decided to make an ice cream run. No big deal, right? We got double cones and then drove down by the lake just to talk and catch up and stuff. We walked out to the end of the dock, took off our shoes, dangled our feet in the water just like a couple of kids, and chatted away. But somehow, we started splashing each other with our feet. Just goofing around, it seemed.

But the next thing I knew, we're really going at it, kicking up water and screaming and laughing, and I thought I was actually getting the best of him. So then he grabbed me, and before I knew what hit me, we're both in the water, still laughing hysterically. And then we got quiet. I remember looking up at him and thinking how, even sopping wet, he looked totally handsome with his dripping blond hair hanging into his eyes—and maybe it was the lake, but his eyes seemed bluer than ever.

And suddenly—I can't even remember exactly how it happened—he kissed me! And I was TOTALLY kissing him back! Right there in the water.

Oh, man! Even as I write this, my face is burning with embarrassment and well, who knows what else? But I knew it was wrong. And he knew it was wrong. But the truth is, we didn't stop kissing right away. And when we did finally stop, there was just this dead silence. All we could hear was the lapping sound of the lake and crickets chirping. We climbed out of the water and both sat there stunned and humiliated, and I'm sure a little breathless. I know I didn't know what to say, and I suppose I felt like it was all my fault somehow. I mean, hadn't I been the one to start splashing in the first place?

"I'm sorry," he told me in a quiet voice.

"I'm sorry too," I echoed back, feeling slightly numb inside.

"Guess we better go now."

I nodded. Then we both stood and tried to shake off the water, which was drying fast thanks to the heat. Then we walked back to his Jeep without even speaking.

We didn't even talk as he drove me home. He apologized again at my house, and I just nodded and walked away, feeling like a total fool. What would Beanie and Jenny think if they knew? I wondered if I would ever tell them (as it turned out, I didn't). And even now that makes me feel like a hypocrite. But I immediately went up to my room and got down on my knees and prayed.

It had been more than a year since I first made my commitment to God not to date. And the main reason I made that promise was because of the way things had gone between Josh and me—it's like we could never keep our hands off each other when we were going out.

So anyway, I told God I was really sorry and that I was wrong. I asked Him to forgive me, and I know that He did. But I must admit it took me a while to really forgive myself. Some people would think this is nothing, but to me it was something. I felt I'd disappointed God—and myself. Still, I reminded myself that I'm human and God doesn't expect me to be perfect—just to be changing daily and becoming more like Him. So I pretty much tried to forget about it. In fact, this is the first time I've given it much thought since then.

Josh e-mailed me that same night, saying once again how sorry he was and how it would never happen again. He also promised to make sure we didn't set ourselves up for that kind of situation again.

But even now I am humbled to think how susceptible I was (and still am) to that sort of thing. To be perfectly honest, I think I had some sort of misplaced pride (like I was above falling into that kind of trap again), but God showed me differently—I'm simply human. And I think it was the same for Josh.

The good thing is, as summer progressed, we did avoid falling into that kind of temptation again. And I believe our friendship deepened and grew. As long as Josh wasn't telling me what to do (in that superior way he sometimes has), we got along fine. Even Chloe mentioned (just last week) how cool it was to see a guy and a girl who could be such good friends without being all romantically involved. I do plan to set her straight on some parts of that theory though—without incriminating her brother, that is. I mean, it is possible for guys and girls to be "just friends," but you have to keep a pretty close eye on things to succeed at it. Unless you're a saint, which I certainly am not!

two

Thursday, September 5 (roommate from ???)

This morning was registration, and I set my alarm early to make sure I got there in plenty of time to get the classes I needed. As it turned out, I did, for the most part anyway. Unfortunately, my English class was already full, so I have to take it on Tuesday evenings at six. I didn't really want a night class, but the good news is that I only have to go to it once a week. At least that's something.

I was surprised that my roommate still hadn't made an appearance by last night. In fact, I felt a little worried that she might've missed registration altogether, but it seems she got here this morning and registered just before it closed. That's cutting it pretty close, but I'll keep these thoughts to myself. I sense Elizabeth (or Liz as she likes to be called) wouldn't care what I think anyway.

Let me describe Liz. She's a tall brunette and kind of big-boned, not heavy though. In a way she reminds me of Minnie Driver, except she doesn't have that same sweet smile. Liz's smile (well, the only one I've seen so far) is much more cynical looking. Kind of a knowing smile, like she thinks she's seen a lot more than everyone else—particularly me. And I could tell right off the bat that she's really sarcastic and skeptical. It's hard to categorize Liz (and I don't really like doing that anyway), but after our brief encounter today, I guess I'd call her an intellectual realist with a great big chip on her shoulder. Okay, I know that's not fair and is probably judgmental, but it's my first impression. And this is a diary to record my honest feelings.

"Oh, you're here," she said with obvious disappointment right after she burst into my room. (I'd already gotten to thinking of it as "my" room and felt slightly stunned to have a stranger just walk right in without even knocking.) "Are you Caitlin O'Conner?" And the way she said my name sounded like she was talking to a little girl.

I stood up, trying to hide my surprise. I smiled and stuck out my hand. "Yes. Are you Elizabeth?"

Next came a half smile and weak handshake. "Yeah. My friends call me Liz." There was a slight pause as she carefully looked me up and down, taking in my striped sweater, worn jeans, and pink bunny slippers (which had never embarrassed me until now). And suddenly it's like I knew what she was thinking—like she was mentally replaying every dumb blonde joke she'd ever heard, like she immediately assumed that due to my looks I was nothing more than a superficial airhead. And I resented it.

"I suppose you can call me Liz too."

I could hear the obvious disdain in her voice. I'm sure she meant for me to hear it, but I still tried not to appear too flustered. "I, uh, I was worried something might be wrong," I began as she turned her back to me and dumped a couple of duffel bags onto her bed. "You didn't miss registration, did you—?"

"First off, Caitlin—" she turned around and again spoke in a way that made me feel as if I were about five years old—"I don't expect you to think you need to keep tabs on me. I don't need a sister or a mother or a baby-sitter. Understand?"

I'm sure I must've blinked and stepped back. "Sure."

"And just because we're roommates doesn't mean we have to be all buddy-buddy, sharing secrets, giggling in the middle of the night, that kind of childish tripe. If I'd wanted that crud, I'd have joined a stupid sorority." She eyed me suspiciously. "In fact, you look like you'd fit in just fine with a sorority."

I felt pretty sure this was meant as an insult. "Well, looks can be deceiving." I was really on the defensive now.

She laughed but not with humor. "So, do you get me then? Do you see where I'm coming from? This is just a room that we have to share, that's all. Understand? Capisce?"

"Yeah, sure, that's fine."

"Good." Her face relaxed a little.

Without thinking I spoke again. "But I guess I hoped we could at least be, you know, just casual friends." Okay, big mistake.

She turned back around from her unpacking, with a black leather belt hanging limply in her hand, then looked at me hard—actually it felt like she glared at me, but that could've been an overreaction on my part. "Do you mind if I'm blunt with you, Caitlin?"

"No, of course not." But to be honest I was worried she might actually walk over and smack me with her belt.

"I don't have many friends. But it's for a good reason. You see, I think that only shallow people fill their lives with too many friends and acquaintances. I, on the other hand, choose my friends very judiciously."

I think I said, "Oh," or something else equally impressive.

"So, if you don't mind, I'd like to unpack in peace."

"No problem." I grabbed my backpack and headed for the door. "I was on my way to the bookstore anyway—"

"Caitlin. You don't have to tell me where you're going. Don't you get it? We don't have to check in with each other. Let's be adults here."

"Sorry."

"Don't be."

Well, let me tell you I got out of there as quickly as possible. And immediately a flood of emotions tumbled through me. The old Caitlin (the-before-I-knew-God Caitlin) was screaming: "What a complete jerk! What a total idiot! Liz Banks is an absolute moron! How can I possibly room with someone like that?" Another, more logical part of me began to consider the practical steps for switching roommates—should I do it now or wait until next week? Then I even started to wonder if Liz might simply have a really devastating case of PMS!

But fortunately, by the time I was halfway to the bookstore, I began to actually pray about this whole situation. First I asked God <u>why</u> He'd put me in a room with someone like Liz Banks. Then I asked Him if I should seek to change rooms. Finally, I decided to earnestly pray for Liz, and I asked God to lead me in what I was supposed to do next. Even now I'm not totally sure what's best. I mean, I've known some difficult people in the last couple years, but I'm not sure that I've ever met anyone who came across quite as cold and hard as Liz. And this is only the first day! On the other hand, it might just be her natural defenses popping up. I suppose she could actually be feeling somewhat insecure right now. And who knows, there could be a really soft heart underneath that tough facade.

Right now, I'm in the coffee shop (the one Josh recommended) writing all this down in my diary. I think it's helping me to sort out my thoughts.

DEAR GOD, PLEASE SHOW ME WHAT TO DO ABOUT
LIZ. I KNOW YOU LOVE HER AND WANT ME TO LOVE
HER TOO, BUT I THINK IT'S GOING TO BE ONE
TOUGH CHALLENGE. SHE COMES ACROSS AS
PRETTY UNLOVABLE. PLEASE HELP ME. I KNOW YOU
CAN LOVE HER THROUGH ME. JUST LET ME BE
YOUR VESSEL. THANK YOU. AMEN.

Saturday, September 7 (darkness meets light)
Yesterday was filled with a lot of freshman orientation
activities, but it's been a pretty lonely day today. To
be honest, I think I'm slightly homesick. I suppose it'll get
better next week when classes actually start. I plan to
go to church tomorrow (the one Josh told me about),
and hopefully I'll make some friends. Despite what Liz
says, I happen to think friends ARE a good thing. And I'm
not even sure you can have too many.

Speaking of Liz, I had to duck out tonight because
her music was getting to me. It's so dark and hopeless
and depressing—all these lyrics about pain and lost love
and futility. And even though she doesn't play it all
that loud, the bleakness started wearing on me.
Anyway, I'm at the library right now and just went on-line
hoping to find some encouraging bits of e-mail from
friends or family—but there's nothing! All I had in my in
box was a couple pieces of smutty spam and an ad from
a credit agency. I suppose everyone else is too busy to
write to me right now. I imagine them all having a good

time, getting together with friends, sharing a few laughs. And I must admit to having to fight down some real waves of jealousy.

Okay, I know I'm right where God wants me. But why does it feel so dark and lonely here? Why did I land such a miserable roommate? And what am I supposed to do about it?

Suddenly this song is hitting me—"This Little Light of Mine"—and I know it's kind of juvenile, but it's making me smile. I remember how we'd sing it in Spanish with the little kids down in Mexico, holding our fingers up like little torches and repeating over and over how we were going to let it shine everywhere.

So I guess that'll be my theme song for right now. Pretty mature for a college coed, eh? But on the other hand, I think it's just what I need. Anyway, I'm heading back to the dorm, and I'll be singing that song all the way there. Then I may put on a good CD of my own— quietly, of course. I don't want to irritate my roomie. Not too much anyway.

Sunday, September 8

I couldn't believe Pastor Obertti's sermon today. It was about being a light in the darkness! It's as if God wanted to confirm that my little song was truly from Him last night and that I really AM right where He wants me to be. Even though my roommate seems to be pretty dark, I can still be a light to her. God wants me to be His

light, and I'm not to hide under anything. I feel so encouraged. Well, mostly anyway.

Unfortunately, I feel a little discouraged to learn
that, due to conflicts at the church, the college fellowship group has changed their meeting time from
Wednesday nights to Tuesday nights (the same night as
my English class!). I doubt there's any chance of changing my class since it looked like everything was full when
I got that one. Still, I'll give it a try tomorrow.

Liz, after sleeping in, has been gone all afternoon,
which I must admit is something of a relief. It's not that I
don't want to be a light to her today (because I do), but
it's nice to have the room to myself for a few hours—
kind of like I'm getting my bearings back. I've been reading my Bible and praying and listening to CDs...sort of
strengthening myself to hopefully be a light for Him.

Another bright spot in my day was having my mom
call me earlier this evening. I never would have
expected to be so happy to hear her voice. But I was. I
even got a little weepy when it was time to hang up,
although I didn't let on. I didn't want her to think that I
wasn't handling everything and being mature. Anyway,
she told me all the latest news. Aunt Stephie's so big she
can hardly move around, and it looks as if she could go
into labor any day. And Pastor Tony (who's usually so cool
and calm) is acting just like any other nervous, first-time
father-to-be. My brother Ben got picked for second-
string quarterback for Leeland Middle School's eighth-
grade team and wants me to let Josh know ASAP. (Josh

had practiced with him a lot this summer.) And of course Mom asked about my new roommate.

"Well, she's kind of different," I told her.

"Different?" I could hear a slight twinge of panic in my mom's voice, as if she was imagining me rooming with some Satan worshiper or drug dealer or something else equally abhorrent.

"It's not like she's into drugs or self-mutilation or anything weird," I reassured her. "But she's not exactly friendly, you know."

"Oh, maybe she's just shy, Caitlin. Remember how shy you used to be back in middle school?"

"Yeah." I nodded grimly. "Maybe that's it."

"You should try to be more outgoing to her, Catie. She probably just needs a good friend."

I kept my thoughts to myself regarding the "friend" topic, then listened as Mom filled me in on a few more things before she said she had to go and prepare some lesson plans for school. After I hung up the phone, I imagined my family going about their normal Sunday evening business. Mom with her first-grade lesson plans, Ben frantically trying to catch up on whatever homework he'd put off all weekend, and my dad at his computer or maybe watching a ball game. Except it was so strange to think that I was the one who was missing from the picture. I mean, usually when I've been away from home, I'm so busy and wrapped up with my own life that I don't take time to even consider what it might be like without me there.

I'll really be glad when classes start tomorrow. Speaking of which, it's getting late. And despite my plan to be God's "little light" for Liz this evening, I think it's going to have to be lights-out for me. I have to get up early for an eight o'clock class in the morning.

THREE

Thursday, September 12

Can people actually undergo a person-
ality change without even realizing it? It's like I'm suddenly turning into someone else. Okay, not really, but sort
of. I'm sure it has to do with being on my own and in a
new place. Also I've been pretty busy with classes and
homework, plus trying to adjust to my somewhat strange
roommate. But somehow I feel like I'm not the same old
Caitlin—and it worries me.

Maybe I feel different simply because I'm no longer
surrounded by my old friends and family. Sort of like
I've been cut loose and set adrift amid this rolling sea
that just carries me away. Of course, I know that God
is here with me, and I believe He's at work, probably
doing something totally amazing with my life. But my
feelings right now seem slightly confused and unsettled.
I'm sure it's because my old surroundings (friends and

family) provided a kind of insulating culture for me. I could count on them to be there for me. And even when we didn't see eye to eye, I knew they still loved me. Here at college, it's as if all the rules have changed. At least that's how it feels.

For one thing, my classes are so huge that I feel all but invisible, like it wouldn't even matter if I didn't show up. After the first week, some teachers don't even take roll call anymore—like they don't even care if you're there or not. But then I guess that's part of this whole adult responsibility thing—we're supposed to be mature enough to do what's right whether or not anyone else notices.

In a way I think I'm lucky that God's been teaching me about this stuff already. And I feel kind of sorry for Liz because she's slept in and been late for a couple of classes already. (The only reason I know this is because I sneaked a peek at her schedule, which she left on top of her desk.) I know she has an eight o'clock class on Tuesdays and Thursdays. But did I interfere and wake her up? You better believe I did NOT! And although my morning class wasn't until ten, I got up even before she did. I showered and then dressed quietly, gathered my things, and went down for breakfast.

Josh was right about the dorm food. Although I've discovered if I get to the dining room early enough, I can get my hands on a yogurt and orange juice, which suits me just fine.

Speaking of Josh, I finally got an e-mail from him

yesterday. I'd written him to let him know I wouldn't be making the fellowship group because of my class. He said that was too bad but to make sure I go next term. Then he told me a little about Bible college. It sounds very cool, like they have this real sense of spiritual family and mission and stuff. And once again I'm trying not to be envious. I mean, I'm really glad for him that he's there, but when I hear these things, it makes me feel sort of left out in the cold.

Which makes me think of Beanie and Jenny and Anna. I also got an e-mail from Beanie (about time!), and it sounds like those three are totally loving their new school. I wrote back and tried to sound equally happy and positive about the university, but I think Beanie will be able to read between the lines. She's always seen right through me. I really wish they could come over here for a visit—which I know is ridiculous, not to mention impractical. Sheesh, here it is just the first week of college, and I miss them all so much. I'm thinking how much I took for granted our time together in high school. What was I thinking? Right now, I wouldn't mind at all going back there. I can just imagine being in the old cafeteria, hanging with my friends... Okay, Caitlin, quit your dreaming! Time to wake up and do your homework.

Friday, September 13 (rude awakening)
Liz and I hardly crossed paths all week. Until this afternoon, that is. I finished my last class and came "home."

(I'm trying to start calling this place home, although it's a real stretch of my imagination.) Anyway, I decided to take a nap. For some reason I felt totally exhausted (another thing that's not usually like me). But I figured it was my first week at college with classes and maybe I was just plain tired.

Anyway, it seems like I've barely drifted off to sleep when suddenly I hear this loud bang, and Liz throws her backpack on the bed and is just cussing up a blue streak.

I jump out of bed, disoriented and still half asleep. "What's going on?"

"I thought I was alone!"

"Are you okay?"

Another string of off-color words that end in: "none of your blankety-blank business."

"Fine!" I say, not bothering to hide my irritation. "Then if you don't mind I'll go back to sleep." Of course, by now I'm wide awake and feeling fairly chagrined (don't you love that word?). But Liz keeps stomping around, making noise and cussing, though somewhat more quietly. All of which is really disturbing.

Finally I sit up and say, "What in the world is wrong with you?"

She sits down on her bed, folds her arms and crosses her legs, and scowls at me as if I've personally done something detestable, which I'm pretty sure I haven't.

"Not that it's any of your business, but if you must know, Rachel is going out with Jordan."

Well, I know from taking phone messages that Jordan is Liz's guy friend, although I'm not sure if they are very serious or not.

"Who's Rachel?" I ask, knowing I might be letting myself in for all kinds of trouble.

"My supposedly best friend."

Well, now I must literally bite my tongue to keep from reminding Liz about how she "judiciously chooses her friends." Instead, I just say, "Oh."

Liz studies me carefully then shakes her head. "I should've known something bad was going to happen today."

"Why?"

She looks at me as if I'm really dumb. "It's Friday the thirteenth."

I nod, trying to think of something encouraging to say. Finally it hits me. "You know, I used to believe in stuff like that too."

Liz groans now, rolling her eyes. "Okay, here it comes."

"What?"

"The big salvation sermon, right?"

"The what?"

"You don't honestly think I haven't noticed your goody-goody Jesus posters and religious music or your Bible always lying open on your bed? Do you really think I'm that dense, Caitlin?" As usual, she says my name like I'm five. "I don't even know why I told you about Jordan and Rachel in the first place." Now she's standing and jerking her arms into her leather coat. "It's like an open invitation for you to start trying to push your Sunday school religion right down my throat."

"I wasn't—"

But it's too late, she was already out the door. Even now I can still hear the slam ringing in my ears.

Of course, I've been praying for her tonight. And I know she's not happy. But at the same time I'm wondering, is it right for her to make me so miserable? Maybe I should see about switching roommates on Monday.

DEAR GOD, PLEASE SHOW ME WHAT TO DO. I DON'T WANT TO TAKE OFF RUNNING WITH MY TAIL BETWEEN MY LEGS JUST BECAUSE LIZ IS HAVING TROUBLES. BUT AT THE SAME TIME, I'M NOT SURE THAT I CAN BE OF ANY HELP TO HER. I FEEL LIKE SHE HATES ME. PLEASE HELP ME TO FOLLOW YOU NOW. AMEN.

Saturday, September 14

I slipped out of my room this morning and walked over to the library to do homework while Liz was still asleep. She came in really early this morning (around 3 a.m.), and I don't expect she'll be up until this afternoon. The pungent smell made it pretty obvious that she'd been drinking. Hopefully she didn't make herself sick.

I feel really bad for her, but I don't know what to do about it. I can't see how my rooming with her is really going to change anything. I mean, people don't change if they don't want to. And I'm pretty sure she doesn't want to. Still, I'm not sure that God wants me to abandon her yet either. More than ever, I'm praying that He'll show me what to do.

I got a sweet e-mail from Josh's sister Chloe today. I'd written her a quick note last week and found myself telling her a little bit about Liz. It's funny that I did because I haven't told anyone else much of anything about my weird roommate. But for some reason, even though Chloe's only fifteen, I just suspected she'd under-stand. I guess in some ways Liz reminds me a little bit of Chloe. Although Chloe is much, much softer and, I think, much closer to accepting Jesus into her heart.

Anyway, Chloe's response was so encouraging. She said that she thinks Liz probably really needs me and that even though Liz won't likely admit it, she may be glad (underneath it all) that I'm her roommate. Then Chloe added, "You know, I think God really does work in mysteri-ous ways." This was very interesting, coming from Chloe, and it gives me more hope for her than I've ever had before.

So I wrote back a long e-mail telling her all about Liz's latest explosions, and now I'm curious to hear what Chloe's reaction will be to that. It makes me feel a little silly though, as if I'm going to a fifteen-year-old (who's not even a believer yet) for advice. But that's not really how it is. I'm mostly just trying to keep the lines of commu-nication open with her. I know that God's up to something in her life, and I really care about her. Not only that, it's nice to be able to be completely candid and honest with someone who won't: 1) get all worried about you, 2) give you a sermon, or 3) tell you to find a new roommate. For now I think Chloe makes a good confidant when it comes to my situation with Liz. In the meantime, I'm praying a lot! And that's a good thing.

Tuesday, September 17

I cannot believe I've been on campus for two weeks and have yet to make a real friend. I've met a couple girls in my dorm who go to my church, and they seem nice and friendly and all, but somehow I just didn't quite hit it off with them. Kind of like we're out of sync or something I can't quite put my finger on. I suppose I'm even wondering if Liz's philosophy for picking friends might not be rubbing off on me. Although, I can't say much for her taste in friends.

I met Rachel (the boyfriend thief) yesterday. Apparently they've patched things up, and now Jordan's the one out in the cold. But to be honest, Rachel seemed a little flaky to me. I had expected someone more like Liz—more intellectual and opinionated. Although, I suppose Liz likes having friends around who don't challenge her authority since she has to be right about absolutely everything. In fact, I even got to witness her and Rachel getting into it over what time a certain TV show was playing. Of course, Liz won the battle, but only because Rachel backed down. I can imagine how the fur must've flown when they were into it over a boy.

I'll have to give Rachel this though—she's a lot friendlier than Liz. She actually asked me where I was from and if I liked school. It was funny too, because it seemed as if Liz's ears perked right up, like she was actually a little curious herself, although she's never bothered to ask me before. Then Rachel told me where they were from and how they'd met in high school and had been friends for a few years.

"How come you guys didn't room together?" I asked (stupidly as it turned out). I saw Liz's eyes flash and Rachel grew uncomfortable.

"Go ahead and tell her," snapped Liz.

"I'm rooming with Gwen." Rachel looked at the floor.

"Oh." I avoided the temptation to ask who the mysterious Gwen might be but assumed it must be the third friend whose presence had most likely forced Liz to room with a stranger. Can't say that I blame Rachel for picking Gwen, whoever she is, over Liz. For I'm sure Liz must be wearing, even on her carefully chosen friends!

Still, even though I write this "tongue in cheek," so to speak, I must admit that I'd really like to have a good friend here with me now. I know I have God, and that's no small thing, but I could use a good, solid Christian friend as well. So I'm specifically praying that God will cross my path with someone really special this week. I'm believing that He will!

Sunday, September 22 (friends!)

God answered my prayer! Not in the way I'd expected, but who am I to complain? I went to church as usual today, and because I was a few minutes early I decided to sit near the front. For some reason, I never mind sitting close to the front. I found a pew that was empty and just sat down. Shortly before the service began, a couple of guys slid in next to me. They looked to be college-aged, and I turned and smiled and they smiled back. Then when it was time for introductions, we exchanged names and I figured out that they'd been good buddies of Josh. As it turns out, Stephen had actually been Josh's roommate last year, and he acted as if he already knew me. To be honest, I couldn't remember Josh talking much about Stephen, but it felt good to know that Josh had talked to him about me. The other guy, Bryce, was a little quieter but seemed nice. After church, they asked if I wanted to join them for lunch and I happily agreed.

Okay, I'd expected that God would send me my first good college friends in the form of girls, but who am I to question God? And it's not like these two guys and I are going to get romantically involved. I know there's not the slightest chance of that. How do I know? Well, Stephen just isn't my type. I mean, he's a sweet guy in a young John Candy kind of way, but I can't imagine the two of us ever getting involved. And although I think Bryce is nice looking enough, he has a girlfriend already, and I have absolutely no interest anyway. And so, for now, I'm just glad to have two new friends. I told them about my English class being on the same night as the fellowship group.

"That's too bad," said Stephen. "But sometimes we get together for other things. We'll have to keep you posted about what's going on."

"We have an early morning prayer group on Fridays," offered Bryce. "It's just guys right now, but I heard a couple girls want to join us. You'd be welcome. We pray for the entire campus."

"That sounds great. Maybe I could get some prayer for my roommate." Suddenly I felt I'd stepped over a line.

"What's wrong?" asked Stephen.

"Oh, nothing really," I said quickly. "But she's not saved. I'm sure she could use our prayers."

"You're rooming with a nonbeliever?" Bryce's eyes got wide. "Do you think that's wise?"

"Well, I didn't really have much control over it." I tried to sound light. "And who knows, maybe God will do a miracle. It wouldn't be the first time, you know."

Stephen laughed. "Yep, you sound just the way Josh used to describe you as."

"And how's that?" I eyed him curiously.

"Oh, he used to call you a spiritual firecracker."

We all laughed.

"Well, I'm not so sure about that. But I'll take it as a compliment."

So I hung out with Stephen and Bryce for the rest of

the day and even went to the evening church service with them. And, believe me, it was the best day I've had since coming to the university. It really gives me hope!

THANKS, GOD, FOR BRINGING THESE TWO FRIENDS MY WAY. THANKS FOR GIVING ME SUCH A FUN DAY. PLEASE HELP ME TO BE A BETTER LIGHT FOR LIZ AND ANYONE ELSE I MEET. AMEN.

FOUR

Thursday, September 26 (out in the cold!)

Grrrr! I am so totally furious that I can barely write! But maybe if I vent a little I'll manage to calm down some. So take a deep breath, Caitlin. Easy does it, girl. Remember God is in control, right?

Okay, just when I thought things were starting to smooth out, it feels like someone jerked the rug out from under me again. Liz had been making herself pretty scarce this week, and even when she was around, it hadn't been quite as toxic as before. I was actually starting to think perhaps I could handle this whole thing after all. As it turns out, the reason she was in better spirits was because she and Jordan were getting back together. Apparently he was sorry for "cheating on her" with Rachel and actually brought by some flowers and a poem in hopes that they might patch things up. I felt a little unsure about accepting these items on Liz's behalf—worried that she might get mad at me—but what could I do? It was actually a pretty nice bouquet, and judging by Liz's reaction, the poem must've hit the spot. So you'd think everything should be just peachy, right? Wrong!

At around seven o'clock Liz informs me that Jordan's on his way over so they can talk this whole thing over tonight, and would I mind making myself scarce for an hour or two? Well, I'm not too excited about getting thrown out of my own room, but I keep these feelings to myself as I toss my stuff together and trek off (in the rain!) to go study in the library. But once I'm there, I wonder why I didn't suggest they go somewhere else to talk it over. Why am I turning into such a little wimp lately? But I know the answer is simple enough: Liz is so overbearing that I'm afraid to stand up to her. And I know my chances of having peace are greater when she is appeased. Pretty stupid, but true.

Finally, it's after nine o'clock, and I'm tired. So I trudge back home, getting soaked all over again. But when I get to my room, I realize that I left in such a hurry earlier that I forgot to grab my keys. I can still see them just sitting on my desk. So I knock on the door, and although I'm pretty sure I can hear whispering, no one answers.

"It's me, Liz. I forgot my key; let me in."

Now I hear suppressed giggles—Liz and Jordan—like this is some big joke. But no one comes to the door. I knock even louder this time. "It's late and I'm tired, Liz. Please, let me in."

But still she doesn't open the door. Now I'm feeling a mixture of anger and humiliation. I feel like an idiot for walking off without my keys, but even so, that's no reason for her to act this way. What are those two doing in there? The thought of them—well, getting physically intimate—in MY room is just way over the top! I mean, I don't actually know if that's what's going on, but on the other hand, I wasn't born yesterday!

Anyway, the whole thing is just too much for me, and I eventually stomp back downstairs to the lobby and flop down on the vinyl couch. Where I am still sitting now. So, do I just spend the night down here—cold and damp and enraged—or do I keep bugging Liz until she lets me in? I know that if I make her mad, she'll make me miserable. And I'm not sure I want to risk that—not just yet anyway—although part of me simply doesn't care. And now I feel completely certain that I want a new roommate, and that she should be the one to move out. But most of all, I feel confused and tired and just plain lost. What would Jesus do under these same circumstances? Turn the other cheek? Sleep on the couch? What?

DEAR GOD, WHY AM I GOING THROUGH THIS? HAVE I DONE SOMETHING WRONG? ARE YOU TRYING TO TELL ME SOMETHING? SHOULD I SEE ABOUT SWITCHING ROOMMATES NOW? PLEASE, SHOW ME

WHAT TO DO BECAUSE I DON'T THINK I CAN TAKE TOO MUCH MORE OF THIS. AMEN.

Friday, September 27

Well, Liz found me in the lobby this morning and acted all surprised and even just a tiny bit sorry.

"What are you doing down here?" she asked with feigned innocence.

"W-what time is it?" I stammered, thinking I must've been late for my first class since Liz never got up early.

She shrugged. "Didn't you know the door was unlocked?"

I looked at my watch to see it was only six. I peered at Liz suspiciously. "Last time I tried the door it was nearly midnight," I said in a flat voice.

"We must've fallen asleep."

I glared at her but said nothing.

"Jordan went home just after midnight, and I left the door unlocked all night long. I thought you'd let yourself in. That's too bad you forgot your key."

"Too bad for me, you mean." I narrowed my eyes. "Came in pretty handy for you."

She rolled her eyes at me. "You're acting like I planned the whole thing, Caitlin. It's not my fault you walked off without your key. Just because we share a room doesn't mean I have to take care of you."

I grabbed my backpack and started to head up, then realized I still didn't have a key. I turned and looked at Liz. "Are you going back up?"

She smiled in a smirky way. "Yeah, I just thought I better check on you."

"I thought you said you didn't have to take care of me."

She flipped a long dark strand of hair over her shoulder. "I don't."

We didn't speak on the way up, and as soon as we got to our room, Liz crawled right back into bed. I wished I could do the same but knew I'd never get up in time to make it to class. Instead I took a quick shower, then hurried over to the early morning prayer meeting that Stephen and Bryce had told me about. I was a little late, but no one seemed to notice. And to my relief, there were a couple of other girls there too. I briefly met them afterward (Sarah and Ashley) and found out they live in a dorm on the other side of campus. I asked them if they knew anyone looking for a roommate, but they didn't. We exchanged phone numbers, then I had to rush off to my first class.

Somehow, I don't feel quite as angry about the whole locked-out thing as I did last night. Maybe it was the prayer meeting or the fact that Liz came down to the lobby to find me or maybe I'm just getting worn down. I don't know.

It does strike me as slightly odd, however, that I, Caitlin O'Conner, am once again sitting all alone in my room on a Friday night. This isn't exactly the way I'd imagined my first few weeks of college going. I know I could've (maybe should've) called Sarah and Ashley to see what they're up to tonight. Or maybe I should try being more friendly to the two Christian girls I met here in my own dorm. But somehow I just can't. Or won't. Why is that?

I mean, I know I'm feeling tired after not getting much sleep last night, but then I can remember being tired in high school but still having plenty of energy to hang with Beanie and Jenny and Anna. So what's wrong with me now? I still have the feeling that something in me is changing, and I'm not sure what to do about it. I keep asking God to show me which way to go, who to become friends with and everything, but nothing seems terribly clear to me. It's all kind of foggy.

I suppose the best thing in all of this is the way I'm leaning on God more and more—sometimes it almost feels as if He's all I have—like I'm slowly getting totally cut off from everything else. Is that how it's supposed to be? Or am I making a big mess of everything? I just don't know.

Still, I must admit that I'm relieved to have "my" room to myself tonight (so far anyway). And I do plan to have a little talk with Liz about having "guests" in our room and hopefully establish some rules we can both agree on. Also, I don't think I'll ever walk off without my key again! As far as switching roommates...I'm still not sure what to do. Part of me is fed up and more than ready to move on. But another part (and I'm afraid it's the part that's listening to God) feels like there may be a reason for this relationship. I guess only time will tell.

Tuesday, October 1

The last few days have passed somewhat uneventfully
(for which I should be relieved). Liz and I talked about
guest rules, and she was surprisingly agreeable. I told
her how it makes me uncomfortable for her to have
Jordan visiting late at night, and she assured me that it
wouldn't be a regular thing.

"I don't want it to be a thing at all," I said firmly.

She pressed her lips together. "Well, I suppose that's
fair."

I tried not to register surprise.

"Besides, if everything works out, you might have this
room to yourself before long."

"Really?" I tried not to sound too hopeful.

"Yeah, Jordan and I are talking about getting a
place of our own."

Now, I hated to seem like I was happy about the idea
of the two of them sharing a room (because I know it's a
bad idea), but at the same time, I was thrilled at the
idea of getting rid of Liz. So I just dumbly nodded my
head without saying anything.

"The only problem is with our folks. Since they're paying our tuition and everything..." Her voice trailed off.
"But you could help me, Caitlin."

Something about the way she said that sent up a
red flag. "How?" I asked anyway, curious as to what she
was cooking up.

"Well, I'm thinking you could pretend like I still live

here in the dorm with you. If my parents should call, which they rarely do, you could say I'm not here or that I'm in the bathroom, and then you could take down their messages and—"

"What you choose to do with Jordan isn't any of my business," I began, praying that God would help me say this right, "that is, unless you're doing it in my room. But it would go against my personal convictions to lie for you."

She scowled. "I knew you wouldn't help me."

"I can't."

"Jordan's roommate agreed to cover for him."

"That's his choice."

"Fine!" She stood up and grabbed her jacket. "I should've known you're too goody-goody to help me."

I bit my lip, controlling myself from saying something I knew I'd regret. But even as I did, I recalled her little speeches about how we're supposed to act like grown-ups and how we're not expected to help each other out at all. But by now, I realized Liz had her own set of rules, and they can change according to her needs. I can't imagine how it would feel to live that way. I mean, I'll admit that I haven't exactly been a happy camper lately, but I'd much rather be in my shoes than hers.

As a result of our little "disagreement," she's been giving me the silent treatment and staying out late every night. And even though I know it's wrong, I keep secretly hoping that she and Jordan will eventually work out some way to move in together. (GOD, FORGIVE ME!) I can't help but think how it would be so much easier and oh so much more peaceful to live in this room by myself. And then because I feel guilty about hoping for something that I know isn't in Liz's best interest, I find myself praying for her even more (like I think that makes up for it!).

DEAR GOD, PLEASE DO A MIRACLE IN LIZ'S HEART. PLEASE, HELP HER TO SEE HOW MUCH SHE NEEDS YOU. SHOW HER HOW MUCH YOU LOVE HER AND HOW YOU REALLY HAVE A MUCH BETTER PLAN FOR HER LIFE. PLEASE HELP ME TO BE A BETTER LIGHT FOR YOU. I CONFESS I'M SELFISH AND SELF-CENTERED AND NOT REALLY LOVING HER THE WAY I SHOULD. I NEED YOUR HELP! AMEN.

Saturday, October 5 (bummed out)

I have a feeling that I'm depressed. And I'm not sure what to do about it. I'm not even sure if that's what it really is. But it's as if this thick, black cloud is hanging over me. Although I get occasional glimpses of sunshine, it's mostly just gloomy, murky darkness pressing in all around me. Oh sure, I get up in the morning and go to my classes. I come home and do my homework. But that's about it. It's like I'm disengaged or something.

Not only that, but I'm really, really homesick. Not just for my family (although that's a huge part of it) but also for my old friends and high school, even for my old bedroom. I just want the good old life I used to live back before I got my stupid "independence." And, believe me, admitting this makes me feel like a great big crybaby, but it's as if I need to say it and just get it out into the open, even if it's only in my diary.

I can't even talk to anyone about how I feel because I'm sure they'd all just laugh at me or think I'm nuts. I pray about this whole thing, and even though it seems to help (at least for a while), these unhappy feelings keep coming back.

It's like I'm not even me anymore. What happened to that Caitlin O'Conner who was always on the go, always thinking she could do anything, go anywhere, ready to change the world? I just don't get it. Oh, I suppose I could pretend to be like the old me, especially if, say, my old friends happened to stop by unexpectedly (like that'll ever happen!). But I'm not even sure I could pull that off. It's as if something in me is broken and I don't know how to fix it.

I even went on-line and looked up the symptoms for depression, and while I don't have all of them, I do have some. I feel tired and apathetic. I don't have much appetite and it's hard to get up in the morning. I feel like I'm not interested in much of anything. I know I don't like the way I feel, but I'm just not sure what to do about it or even if I _can_ do anything. But here's what scares me the most—I'm starting to remind myself of Liz!

DEAR GOD, PLEASE HELP ME. I THINK SOMETHING'S WRONG, BUT I DON'T EVEN KNOW EXACTLY WHAT IT IS. PLEASE GIVE ME SOMEONE TO TALK TO,

SOMEONE WHO'LL UNDERSTAND AND KNOW HOW
TO HELP. I KNOW YOU'RE HERE WITH ME AND THAT
YOU LOVE ME, BUT I FEEL SO ALONE RIGHT NOW.
PLEASE, HELP. AMEN.

Sunday, October 6

Somehow I dragged myself out of bed this morning.
(When all I really wanted to do was to sleep in and forget about everything—especially my miserable little life.)
Liz never made it back last night, and I must confess
that it hardly concerned me at all. Mostly I was grate-
ful to have the room to myself as I slowly and ploddingly
dressed for church. Then I walked through the chilly
morning fog, barely noticing the fall foliage that seemed
to have changed color overnight. It's as if part of me was
dead—or dying.

When I got to church I couldn't force myself up into
the front pews, so I sat in the back, hunkering down, my
Bible in my lap, hoping to meld into the seat and disap-
pear. Yes, I was definitely in bad shape.

Just before the service started, Bryce slipped into
the pew beside me. I glanced up at him and tried to
smile, but I'm sure it must've looked pathetic. He
appeared slightly surprised to see me there, and I knew
he hadn't sat by me intentionally. I suppose that made
me feel even worse. I didn't look his way again throughout the entire service.

I'm not totally sure when I began to tune in to what

Pastor Obertti was saying—was it midway through the sermon or closer to the end—but it was the words: "You must die to yourself daily" that really caught my attention. Suddenly I sat up straighter and even leaned forward, hoping that I might somehow absorb the meaning of what he was saying.

"Jesus laid down His life for you," he continued. "Not so you could live a perfectly wonderful life, but so you might, in turn, lay down your life for Him. Jesus said that whoever tries to gain his life will lose it, and whoever willingly gives up his life, for His sake, will gain it."

Let me tell you, those are not easy words to hear. Even when the service ended, I found myself sitting in the pew and mulling over the pastor's sermon. It felt as if a huge battle was waging inside my chest, and I didn't even notice that tears streamed down my face. I just stared into my lap, studying the blurry words on the front of my Bible, trying to pray but not really succeeding. You know how it feels when you have a great big lump in your throat? Well, I felt like I had a gigantic lump right in my spirit—as if something was blocking me and I didn't quite know what it was.

Just then I felt a nudge on my shoulder and looked up to see Bryce looking down at me.

"Are you okay?" he asked with concerned brown eyes.

I swallowed hard and tried to speak, then just shook my head.

"You wanna talk?"

The truth is, I didn't want to talk to him or anyone

just then, but for some reason I nodded and stood.

"How about a cup of coffee?" he suggested as he ushered me out of the church.

"Sure," I managed to croak. "Sounds good."

I attempted to regain a little composure as we walked to the coffee shop. Fortunately for me, Bryce carried the bulk of the conversation, informing me that Stephen had borrowed his car to go home for the weekend to celebrate his parents' silver wedding anniversary. Then we were seated in the coffee shop and I knew it was my turn to talk. How could I possibly explain what I was feeling to someone I barely knew, especially since I hardly understood the whole thing myself? I took a sip of cappuccino. "You must think I'm a real basket case."

Bryce shrugged. "Who isn't occasionally?"

I studied him more closely. He looked pretty together to me with his neatly cut brown hair, navy sweater, and Gap khakis. By all appearances he was a confident sort of guy who knew exactly who he was and where he was going. Kind of like Josh.

"I don't know what's wrong with me," I said, although I knew that wasn't entirely true.

He nodded and took another sip of coffee.

"Well, I guess I sort of know. For one thing I'm homesick." I glanced up at him, wondering if he'd think I was a big baby, but he just nodded as if he understood. "And I feel sort of lost—like a tiny fish in a big sea." He nodded again. "And on top of that I've managed to get the worst roommate imaginable."

Bryce smiled. "The first year is always hard."

"Was it hard for you?"

He nodded. "Yep. It's easy to admit it now, but I didn't tell a soul at the time. I was so homesick last year that I started getting stomachaches, and it was hard to keep food down."

"Really?"

"Yeah. And I'd come from a small town—well, you know, Campbell. It's only about twenty miles from your hometown."

"Wow, that is small."

"Uh-huh. It's the kind of place where everybody knows everybody. A little different from here."

"Must've been hard."

"It took a couple months to make the adjustment. But I started going to the fellowship group and made some good friends. And now it all seems like a distant memory."

I sighed. "Well, that gives me hope."

"What did you think of today's sermon?"

"It really got to me."

He swirled the coffee around in his cup. "Yeah, me too."

"I know it's probably just what I needed to hear too, but it sure wasn't easy. I guess I felt pretty nailed."

"That's a good way to describe it."

I smiled. "Yeah. To be totally honest, I think I've been having a great big pity party lately. Party of one, that is."

He chuckled. "We've all been there."

"It's like I've been so wrapped up in poor old me and my

miserable little life and how nothing seems to be going right. I think it's gotten me pretty bummed, if not totally depressed."

"That's usually what happens when we focus on ourselves too much."

"Kind of like what Pastor Obertti said about trying to save your life and yet losing it?"

"Yep."

"And I'm even thinking about my roommate now. Like maybe God really did put me with her for a reason, but now I'm worried my self-centeredness may be messing it all up."

"It's not too late. God can fix anything—if you let Him."

"Yeah. I think I'm ready to let Him. It's no fun doing it the other way."

We talked for about an hour, and by the time we finished, I felt so much better. And I felt as if I knew Bryce better too. There's a lot more to him than I'd originally assumed. He's a very thoughtful and sensitive guy, with a real heart for God. He's someone I appreciate having for a friend. And it's such a relief to know that he already has a serious girlfriend. She goes to school out of state, but they've been involved with each other since high school.

"We hardly ever see each other," he explained as we walked toward the dorms. "But we e-mail almost daily, and in some ways that makes us feel closer than when we're actually together."

So I feel like, not only did I make a good friend today, but God got my attention in a big way. Now I'm going to look up (and write down) all those Bible verses about dying to self daily. And I'll try to remember that my life belongs to God <u>not me.</u> If I find myself indulging in a stupid pity party, it must mean that I'm not laying down my life for Him. Because it's hard to feel sorry for yourself when you're living for God.

The cool thing was, as I walked back to my dorm, I actually noticed how totally gorgeous the fall foliage was today. The fog had burned off and the sun was shining through the colorful leaves. They looked just like jewels—amber and rubies and amethysts! It was so amazing. I even gathered a bunch of leaves to take to my room. And you know what? I almost feel like my old self again!

THANKS, GOD! THANK YOU FOR REMINDING ME THAT I AM YOURS AND THAT I'M NOT TO CLING TO MY LIFE BUT TO SIMPLY LAY IT AT YOUR FEET. AND THANK YOU FOR THE FRIEND YOU GAVE ME IN BRYCE TODAY. HELP ME TO REMEMBER ALL THAT YOU SHOWED ME, AND HELP ME TO BE A BRIGHT AND SHINING LIGHT FOR YOU! AMEN.

FIVE

Tuesday, October 8

I've been really trying to reach out to Liz lately. And strangely enough I think I've made some real progress. We actually had a conversation this evening (before she left to meet Jordan). It started when I told her that I'd been a little depressed and homesick last week. I'm not quite sure what made me tell her, except that I was offering her some goodies from a package my mom sent. (I think Mom's mother's intuition kicked in, and she suspected that I'd been feeling bad.)

"Yeah, you seemed bummed," she said as she bit into a homemade chocolate chip cookie. "Not your regular perky self." Although, the way she said the word "perky," it sounded like she might've been referring to a bad skin disease.

"You probably liked that." I forced a smile, hoping she wouldn't take that wrong.

"In case you haven't guessed, I'm not really into perky." She studied me then shook her head. "No offense, Caitlin, but you're the last person I'd have picked to room with."

I tried not to be offended as I offered her another cookie. "Why's that?"

She laughed. But it was that hard, brittle laugh. "Isn't it obvious? We're like the original odd couple, oil mixing with water, Goody Two-Shoes meets Madonna, you know?"

"But you don't really know me—"

"Oh, I know you. Don't kid yourself."

I set down the cookie tin and focused on her. "Nope, I don't think you really do. Sheesh, I hardly know myself some days. But since you think you know me so well, how about if you tell me just who it is you think I am."

She sat down on her bed and studied me, a sly smile playing on her lips. "I don't know... I'm not sure you can take it."

I sat down on my bed across from her, took another cookie, and said, "Try me?"

"Fine." She folded her arms and looked evenly at me. "Well, like I told you that first day, I think you're a good little Christian girl who's been going to Sunday school since you were in diapers. I doubt you've ever done anything seriously wrong. Your parents are probably fine church-going people, respected in the community but slightly hypocritical behind closed doors. You were probably a good student in school but not highly academic;

maybe you were a cheerleader with lots of popular friends who all walked and talked and dressed alike. Your boyfriend was probably a jock who's moved on to bigger and better things, or so he thinks. You're feeling slightly lost just now, like a small duck in a big pond. As a result, you're probably suffering from some real self-esteem issues, and right now, you're probably wishing I'd shut up." She narrowed her eyes. "Am I right?"

Part of me wanted to explode and just tell her off, but at the same time, I knew this was the most conversation we'd had in a month. "Okay," I began slowly, fighting for self-control, "you're about half right—or maybe less." I thought for a moment. "I am a Christian, but it was less than two years ago when I made that commitment. I've never been a cheerleader, and I'm actually fairly academic. I've never been really popular, although one of my friends was, but then she decided that popularity was highly overrated. And my best friend—" I stopped and laughed as I thought about good, old Beanie. "It's ironic, but my best friend is actually a little like you—or she used to be anyway. My parents used to think she was a real wild child because she dressed pretty weird and liked to shock people. She had a pretty sad home situation and then she got pregnant and—" I stopped myself. "You probably don't really want to hear all of this."

Liz was staring at me now, like maybe she thought I was making all this stuff up or something. Then she shrugged. "Well, I guess it just goes to show that you can't judge people based on appearances alone."

I smiled. "But it's easy to do, isn't it?"

"So then, who do you think I am?"

I felt slightly off guard now. Certainly I had my opinions about Liz, but I wasn't really ready to voice them to her. Above all else, I didn't want to hurt her feelings.

"Come on," she urged, "I told you."

"Okay." I peered closely at her smooth, even features, still slightly amazed at how she usually managed to keep her face somewhat emotionless. I suspect she'd be good in a poker game. Then suddenly I wondered what it was that I'd overlooked or possibly misjudged in her, but I decided to begin anyway.

"Well, I'm guessing your family is fairly well off, but I don't think they're very happy. Maybe your parents are divorced. I think it's possible that someone, maybe even someone in your family, has hurt you deeply, and I doubt you've forgiven them for it. I'm sure you're very academic but slightly lazy or perhaps just unmotivated. Maybe you've even depressed; I'm not sure. But I'll bet you don't love Jordan nearly as much as you think you do, and I suspect you don't have one single good friend that you can really count on." I felt my eyes get wide as I realized what I'd just said. I hadn't really meant to go that far. It's like it all came pouring out of me. "I-I'm sorry, Liz," I stammered as I noticed her countenance darken, if only for a moment. Then she just laughed again.

"Hey, don't worry, I can take it. And for your info, you're not even half right. My parents are happily married, and although they're comfortable, I wouldn't describe them as well off. Yes, I am academic, and maybe I am lazy. But then I've never had to work hard to get good grades. As far as that bit about Jordan and my friends—" she rolled her eyes dramatically—"I think your imagination is putting in overtime. Or maybe you're just jealous since I haven't seen you with one single friend." Then she stood up and pulled on her jacket. "Of course, I could be all wrong too." She snatched another cookie from my tin, then jerked open the door. "We could both be all wrong." And then she was gone.

Although it wasn't exactly a feel-good sort of conversation, it was better than nothing, and I do think I know her slightly better now. Not so much by what she said as by the way she said it. She really seemed to react strongly to what I said about Jordan and her friends, which leads me to suspect that, despite her denial, I might not have been too far from the truth. Mostly I think Liz is one mixed-up girl. But I also believe God has a plan for her. And I actually hope I get to be part of it.

Wednesday, October 9 (great news!)

It's pretty late, but I just had to take a moment to write down the great news! I just returned my mom's phone call to find out that Aunt Steph finally went into labor this morning, and Clayton Antonio Berringer was born at 3:50 p.m., weighing in at a sturdy eight pounds and six ounces. Steph and Tony are totally jazzed, and now little Oliver has a baby brother. It's just too cool! My dad already e-mailed the baby's first picture to me. He looks tiny and wrinkly and red, but he has the biggest dark eyes. I just love that they named him for Tony's brother Clay. I bet Clay is looking down from heaven and rejoicing right now. I can't wait to see the baby in person!

Thursday, October 10 (an escape)

Okay, I'm trying really hard not to be mad at Liz for eating all the goodies my mom sent me this week. I mean, I told her to help herself, but I didn't expect her to go hog-wild about it. Anyway, I know it's really petty to get all worked up about something so trivial, especially when I've got something great to look forward to this weekend!

Bryce called tonight to ask if I might possibly want to hitch a ride home with him for the weekend. "I know how much you've been missing your family lately, and I was due for a trip myself—"

"I'd love to go!" I hope I didn't scream in his ear. "My aunt just had her baby yesterday, and I'm dying to see him. I can't believe you called. God must've given you the idea."

So it's all settled; we're leaving tomorrow after my last class, and I should be home in time for dinner. I can't wait! I even e-mailed Beanie, suggesting that maybe they should consider a weekend at home too—like maybe we could have a mini reunion. I haven't heard back yet, but I'm keeping my fingers crossed. I e-mailed Chloe too, since I

owed her one, and told her I'd be around if she wanted
to get together for a cup of coffee or something. Her last
e-mail makes me think she's approaching a real spiritual
crossroads in her life just now, and I'd like to be as available to her as possible.

I've tried to keep a lid on my enthusiasm around here
since Liz seems glummer than usual tonight. I have a
feeling things aren't going too smoothly with Jordan right
now. Maybe that's why she ate all my goodies this
week—stress eating. Anyway, I overheard her talking to
him on the phone earlier. (It's hard not to eavesdrop when
you share a room.) But she was complaining that they
haven't found a place to live yet, and then she ques-
tioned him about how serious he actually was about the
whole moving-in-together thing. Then she got really mad,
cussed at him, and threw the phone across the room. I'm
glad we each have our own phones.

The whole time this was going down, I kept my head
in my computer, pretending to furiously concentrate on a
paper I'd already written that only needed a final proofing. I really wished there was something I could say to
her but sensed my input (right now) would only make
things worse. And even though I feel bad for her, I must
admit that hearing her rant and rave like that makes
my stomach twist and hurt. I had to take some deep
breaths and force myself to relax. Then I really prayed
for Liz (silently, of course). And I pretended not to notice
when she crawled into bed with her clothes still on and
switched off her light. I tried to hurry up and finish my

proofing, then brought my books and journal to the lobby to finish up studying. I didn't really want to go to bed myself since it was only a little past eight.

And I'm glad I came down to the lobby because it gave me a chance to get better acquainted with one of the Christian girls who lives in my dorm. Her name is Kim Murray, and she goes to the fellowship group. Interestingly enough, she was studying downstairs herself because she and her roommate weren't getting along too well either.

"But I thought your roommate was a Christian," I said after she'd told me a little about their argument.

Kim frowned. "Lindsey may be a Christian, but she still has a problem with her temper sometimes."

I laughed. "Well, I guess we're all just human, right?"

"Yeah, and some of us are more human than others."

I wasn't sure how to respond to that and decided not to go there right now. I closed my biology book and leaned back into the couch. Did I really want to get to know Kim better? To be honest, she can come across as a little stuck-up—the kind of girl who holds her head in a certain way, as if to show she's slightly superior to the rest of us.

Kim closed her laptop and slipped it into what looked like a pretty expensive designer bag. "So, why don't you come to the fellowship group on Tuesdays?"

I told her about my night class, then for some reason I decided to ask her about her major. Maybe I was just bored and not ready to go up to my room.

"Social services." She smiled.

Now this took me slightly by surprise. "And why's that?"

"I want to be a social worker."

"What does that mean exactly?" I felt stupid for asking this, because I do know a little about social workers, but I just couldn't imagine the chic Kim doing this sort of work.

"Well, it could actually mean a lot of things, but what I want to do, specifically, is work in international adoption."

"Really?" I looked at this girl with fresh interest. Perhaps I'd been wrong in my first impression. Maybe she wasn't the spoiled, shallow type of girl that I'd imagined. Of course, that's usually the trouble with first impressions. But you'd think I'd have learned that by now.

She nodded. "Did you know there are thousands of homeless children all over the world just waiting to be adopted into loving homes?"

"Actually, I do know a little about it. I've spent a few weeks during the last two summers working at a mission down in Mexico. The main focus of the mission is to reach out to children—either orphans or impoverished." I went on to explain about the kids who live at the garbage dump and how I've worked to raise money to help them.

"That's so cool, Caitlin." Her face brightened into a big smile. "I never would've guessed that you'd care about something like that. It looks as if we have something in common."

"What first made you interested in helping homeless kids?" I asked.

"I was one of them once."

"Really? You were homeless?" I tried not to stare at her expensive clothing and jewelry. I mean, she could've been in an ad for Ralph Lauren or Tommy Hilfiger.

"Yep. I was abandoned on the streets of Seoul, South Korea, in the middle of winter. They figured I was less than six months old at the time, although they never discovered my actual date of birth. A policeman took me to an orphanage that specialized in international adoption. Naturally, I was too little to remember any of this, but I imagine it wasn't very nice, and I didn't look too great. I've seen some pictures—I was skinny and ugly and had these awful open sores on my face when they first took me in. But the orphanage people fed and cared for me and eventually found me a good home here in America. And, well, here I am."

"Wow, I had no idea. That's so cool."

"I know. And last summer I got to take a trip to my homeland and to the actual orphanage and everything. That's when it hit me—I want to give back. I want to help others like me." She leaned forward. "Did you know that they allow baby girls to starve to death in China just because no one wants them?"

We talked until almost ten. Then Kim decided to call it a night, but I stayed down here a little longer to write all this in my diary. I feel so thankful that I got to spend time with this interesting girl. Oh, I don't know if we'll ever become close friends, but it's a possibility. And I just think it's so cool how God brought us together tonight. I wanted to ask her more about her situation with her roommate—like was Kim possibly interested in making a switch? But I suspect that would be a wrong move on my part. Still, you never know.

THANKS, GOD, FOR DOING SOME REALLY GREAT THINGS IN MY LIFE LATELY. IT'S HARD TO BELIEVE THAT JUST A WEEK AGO I WAS SO BUMMED. HELP ME NEVER TO LOSE SIGHT OF YOU, LORD. YOU ARE MY JOY. YOU ARE MY STRENGTH. YOU ARE MY HOPE. I LOVE YOU! AMEN.

SIX

Monday, October 14 (a weekend of R and R)

I had such a great weekend that it was a little hard to come back to school last night. In fact, all day long I've been wondering why I need to go to school here at all. I saw Andrea LeMarsh at church yesterday, and she says community college is just fine. But I know my parents would think that was a real step down for me. So here I am.

But at least this weekend was a brief reprieve. First off, I got to see my new cousin, little Clay. He is such a sweet baby! Steph says he hardly fusses at all, and already he's looking much cuter than the picture Dad sent me. Steph was pretty tired since it was her first day home, so I didn't stay long. But it was so good to see her and Tony and Oliver—it seemed like it had been forever.

And I was just as glad to see my family too! And to

sleep in my own room, although it looks completely different now. My mom's transformed it into her office/hobby room. But my old bed was still there, and that was somewhat comforting. Plus I didn't have to share the room with anyone! We didn't do much on Friday night (after visiting Tony and Steph), but that was just peachy with me. I was happy to be home. Chloe called that same night and asked if I could meet her for coffee the next morning. Her voice sounded different somehow, sort of serious and at the same time slightly mysterious.

So I met her at Starbucks, and to my surprise she looked different. Oh, she still wore the same funny threads, had her dark hair kind of spiky, and had approximately the same number of piercings. But I could tell right off that something about her had changed. It was something in her eyes that gave it away.

"Hey, you look great, Chloe," I said as I gave her a hug. "What's up?"

"Oh, nothing much." But there was an unmistakable twinkle in her eye.

As we ordered our coffee I was suddenly assaulted with the fear that perhaps she'd gotten herself a new boyfriend. I remembered how crushed she'd been the last time she'd gotten involved with a guy and then been dumped. I sure didn't wish that on her just now.

"So how's your first year of high school going?" I already knew that she wasn't liking her new environment too much—another area where we shared common ground of late.

She made a face. "Oh, it's pretty much the same. Too many insecure kids, like me I suppose, all trying to act cool but looking like complete morons just the same."

I laughed. "That sounds about right."

"But there is something..." She took a sip of coffee, peering at me over the heavy mug with what looked like a suppressed grin.

"What?" I set down my cup with a thunk. "I can tell something's up, Chloe, and I'm dying to know. So just spill it, will ya?"

She slowly set down her cup. "I did it."

I studied her face, still unsure where this conversation was headed, and to be honest, I suppose I was actually fearing the worst. "Did what?"

She giggled. And I can say this is the first time I've ever heard Chloe giggle. I mean she's just not the giggly type. In fact, in that same moment, I was keenly aware of how Chloe was a lot like Beanie, and yes, even Liz, I suppose. And it struck me as just slightly ironic that I keep getting paired off with these types of girls. But then maybe it's a God thing.

Chloe leaned forward and looked right into my eyes. "I invited Jesus into my heart."

Well, I'm sure my jaw must've dropped as I absorbed her words. Then I jumped up and hugged her. "Oh, I can't believe it! That's the best news I've heard in weeks. Tell me what happened."

She proceeded to tell me how she'd been reading the Bible (places I'd recommended for her to read—specifically the things Jesus had said). And then she said how she'd actually prayed this week, asking God to show her whether or not He was for real and if the things she was reading were true.

"Well, this is where it gets a little strange," she continued, "but hang with me here. I've probably never told you about how I like to walk around in the cemetery." She paused as if waiting for my reaction, but I nodded like that was the most natural thing in the world. "Well, most people think it's pretty weird—and just slightly morbid. But I like it, and sometimes I've made up some pretty good songs there. Anyway, I went to the cemetery yesterday, just to walk and think. I pretty much did my regular route, except I stopped in an area that I don't usually stop in—probably because it's newer and I tend to like the older sections better. It's like they have more substance or something. Anyway, I sat down on this fairly new cement bench and leaned over to think. I guess I was wondering why God hadn't answered my prayer. I don't know what I'd been expecting. The thing is: I probably expected to be disappointed..." She took a sip of coffee and paused as if considering what she was about to say.

"And?" I couldn't hide my impatience.

"And I looked up at the gravestone, and right there on it were the exact words from one of the last verses you'd sent me—one that I'd been seriously thinking about. It's the one where Jesus says: "I am the way and the truth and the life. No one comes to the Father except through me."

I felt myself gasp just then as it hit me. "Were you—were you at Clay Berringer's grave?"

She nodded her head. "Yeah, and it was so weird because I really didn't know him, and I never even went to his funeral or anything. But I did know he was a friend of Josh's, and yours too. And it seemed so bizarre that I was sitting in front of his grave and reading the same words you'd just e-mailed to me. All of a sudden I got all goose bumpy and actually started to cry, and somehow I knew." She looked at me with what appeared to be tears in her eyes. "I just knew that God was doing the whole thing."

"Oh, Chloe, that is so cool."

She nodded. "And so I did it. I gave my heart to Jesus, right there in the cemetery."

"So how do you feel now?"

She smiled. "Totally great!"

"Have you told anyone?"

She shook her head. "I almost e-mailed Josh yesterday. But when I got the e-mail that you were coming, I wanted to tell you first."

I reached over and squeezed her arm. "I'm so happy for you."

She took a deep breath. "Yeah, I can still hardly believe it myself. I keep thinking maybe I imagined the whole thing. But I really feel different inside. And I've

been praying a lot since then and reading the Bible
even more. I even wrote a couple songs about the whole
thing."

"This is so cool."

Her face grew more serious. "But I'm not sure what to
do next."

I nodded, thinking about it. "Well, praying and reading your Bible are probably the most important things,
but you also need to start having some fellowship." Now,
it was funny as I said this because I was suddenly
aware that I was giving advice that I needed to heed
myself.

"You mean like going to church?"

"Yeah, that's part of it. But you also need to get in
with a group of Christian kids your own age. Is there a
good youth group at your parents' church?"

Her face grew slightly cloudy. "I suppose so..."

"Is there a problem?"

"Oh, I don't know..." She looked down at her coffee. "I
guess the youth leader is sort of...well, he's kind of a yup-
pie type, you know, and I just don't think I'd fit in too
well."

I considered this. "Well, Josh used to go to my youth
group. Maybe you'd like to try it—that is, if your parents
don't mind."

She looked up and grinned. "I think they'll be so happy
to see me involved in church that they won't care where
I go. Well, as long as it's not some form of cult or something
weird." She laughed. "Although I'm pretty sure my dad

thought I was turning into a satanist or something equally frightening."

"Are you going to tell them?"

"Yeah, but I want to tell Josh first. Hey, did you know he's coming home this weekend too?"

"Nope." Despite myself, I felt my heart do that irritating little flutter thing at the mention of his name. "But then I didn't get any e-mail from him this past week. I guess he's been pretty busy with school lately. Maybe you can go to church with him on Sunday."

"Yeah, that sounds like a plan."

Then she asked me how it was going with my roommate, and I filled her in a little, even asking her to pray for Liz. "I think you'd sort of understand her," I said. "Maybe even better than I do—we're as different as night and day."

Chloe smiled. "Just don't underestimate how God uses you, Caitlin. I mean, look at what happened to me after you got involved in my life."

I laughed. "Yeah, I remember the first time I met you and I wondered what in the world we'd possibly have in common."

She giggled. "Yeah, and I thought what's this preppy-looking older chick doing hanging out with the likes of me?"

"But God was really up to something."

Chloe slowly nodded her head as if the whole thing was still just sinking in. "Yeah, I guess He was."

We talked and joked for about an hour before Chloe

had to head off to a baby-sitting job.

"Do you like to baby-sit?" I asked her as we went out the door.

"Yeah, I think little kids are great."

"Then I'll have to introduce you to my aunt. She has a preschooler and a newborn baby, and she just mentioned yesterday how she's looking for a good baby-sitter since all her old reliables took off for college this year."

"Sounds great."

Well, I couldn't help but smile as I drove home from Starbucks. To think that Chloe had given her heart to Jesus while sitting in front of Clay's grave. Only God could do something so totally cool. And then it struck me—I hadn't even told her that my aunt was married to Clay's brother or that this new addition to our family (that I was suggesting she might baby-sit) was actually Clay's nephew and namesake!

As it turned out, Jenny did drive Beanie and Anna home for the weekend, and we all got together on Saturday afternoon. First we went to the mall and just hung out and caught up. Then we decided to pull an all-nighter at Jenny's house. It was so great to see my old friends. And it didn't take too long to learn that everything hadn't been going perfectly smoothly for them either. Anna had gotten a roommate who snores like a logger and lets her laundry pile up until the whole room smells like rotten tennis shoes. And although Beanie and Jenny were used to sharing accommodations, they'd never lived in such close quarters (in the same room),

and even their relationship had begun to wear thin
after the first couple weeks.

"Yeah, we had to start giving each other more
space," explained Jenny as she botched a perfectly good
pool shot.

"But once we figured that out, it's been pretty much
okay."

Anna laughed. "Yeah, except for last week when
Beanie came storming over to my room after she and
Jenny had gotten into a big stink over whose turn it was
to take out the garbage."

"Oh, it wasn't that bad," said Beanie.

So I told them a little bit about Liz, and they all
acted appropriately sorry for me but also promised
they'd be praying for her. And somehow, after hearing
about their less-than-perfect situations, I felt slightly
better about mine. I suppose it's sad but true: Misery
does love company.

Then we all went to youth group and church the
next day. And sure enough there were Chloe and Josh. I
don't think I'll ever forget the smile on Josh's face as he
proudly introduced his sister to the kids in the youth
group—kind of reminded me of how Tony had looked
when he'd introduced me to his new son Clayton Antonio.

And despite how pleased I was for both Chloe and
Josh, I must admit to feeling just a smidgen of what I
think was probably some form of jealousy. Like I should've
been getting some of the credit or glory—I mean, hadn't
I had a hand in helping Chloe reach this place? But at

the same time I chided myself for my stupid selfishness. After all, I know that it was totally God's doing. And what if He had used me? Who am I to strut around like I'm something special? And so I felt adequately humbled, and as a result, I may have seemed more quiet than usual.

"Are you okay?" Josh asked me after the service ended.

"Sure." I smiled brightly.

"Do you have time to grab some lunch?"

I glanced at my watch. "I really wish I could, Josh, but Bryce is picking me up in about ten minutes."

"Bryce Lundgren?"

"Yeah, I almost forgot you know him. He's the one who gave me a ride from school."

A tiny shadow crossed Josh's face. "So you two are pretty good friends, huh?"

I laughed. "Yes, but that's all we are. Y'know Bryce already has a girlfriend."

He nodded, but I could tell he was slightly embarrassed by his line of questioning. "Well, I just wanted you to know how much I appreciate everything you've done for Chloe. God is really using you, Caitlin." He smiled that dazzling Matt Damon smile. "And you just never cease to amaze me."

"Amaze you?"

"Yeah, the way you keep living for God—giving 100 percent. I really admire you. And I thought it was time for me to say it."

Well, I wasn't quite sure what to say, but I think I mumbled a quiet thank-you or something like that. But I must admit that Josh's approval meant a lot to me. Sometimes we forget to tell each other that we're doing a good job. And it was sweet of him to say that to me.

On the way back to school, I told Bryce all about Chloe and her graveyard conversion. He thought the whole thing was pretty cool and promised that he'd be praying for her to stick to her commitment and grow strong in the Lord.

So all in all, it was a fairly amazing weekend. And I came back to school all happy and pumped and ready to let my little light shine!

It just figures that I'd walk into my room to find Liz and Jordan making out—and who knows what else—on top of her narrow bed! I slightly blew it by losing my temper. I threw my bag onto the floor and then said, "Excu-use me!"

Well, they hardly even noticed me standing in the open doorway, fists doubled in anger, as I stared at them. Finally Liz spoke in an exasperated tone, "Can't you just get lost for a little while, Goody Two-Shoes?"

I took in a deep breath and silently counted to ten (okay, I counted pretty fast). "Look, Liz, we had an agreement. And right now you're breaking it. If anyone should get lost for a few minutes it should be you two." I almost couldn't believe my own words—the way I stood up for myself. And it wasn't in anger either. It's like I had an extra measure of self-control—as if God was empowering me. And so I remained in the doorway, silently praying for strength and help, my feet rooted to the floor.

Finally, Liz sat up and glared at me. "Oh, okay," she snarled as she gave Jordan a shove, causing him to tumble to the floor. "Let's get outta here!"

And that's when I knew I was back.

SEVEN

Saturday, October 19

I wasn't too excited about my first midterm week at college, but now I think it was a blessing in disguise since it proved a good distraction from my roommate situation. In an attempt to avoid Liz's hostile and unpredictable mood swings (she and Jordan are fighting again), I buried myself in the books and subsequently feel pretty good about my grades now. But Liz never seems to study, and she doesn't seem a bit concerned about her grades either. How can that be?

But here's what's really bugging me about her (petty as it sounds on paper)—she keeps eating my food. Now I realize I should be more generous and willing to share. And maybe I would be—if she'd just ask first! But, no, she sneaks around while I'm at class or the library or wherever, and like a little mouse (or a big rat!) she gets into the stash that my mom sends me and nibbles away.

This week alone, she's eaten almost all of my Mystic Mints (my favorite store-bought cookies!) and a whole box of Triscuits (that I hadn't even opened), plus she drank most of my Snapples. Okay, maybe it's partly my fault because I've tried to share with her, like when I'm having a snack and she's here, but I haven't let her know how much it bugs me when she just helps herself while I'm gone. And it's funny because she's the one who acts all like: "Oh, I'm so independent and don't need anyone!" and yet it appears she might starve if she didn't have my food. Maybe she should try getting up on time to get some breakfast downstairs!

Okay, enough whining about that. On a brighter note, I had a great e-mail from Chloe today, and it sounds like things are really going well for her. She is so turned on to God! Talk about your night-and-day conversion! But here's what really cracks me up: She keeps saying that no matter how much she changes on the inside, she has no desire to change her outward appearance unless God specifically tells her to. And I say, "Go girl!" Because who knows, maybe God could really use someone who looks like Chloe. I think she could end up reaching a whole different bunch of kids.

In some ways I envy her. I wish I could be more out there in my appearance—and even in my personality. Like Liz (not that I want to be like her), but sometimes I sort of envy the way she just plows through life being her own person—as obnoxious as that can sometimes be. And yet here I am all bent out of shape because I have a hard time asking her to "please, don't eat my cookies." Good grief! I almost make myself sick!

But then I remember that God made me the way He did for a reason. I mean, what would it be like if everyone were the same? Pretty boring I suppose...or perhaps we'd all just kill each other. Anyway, I guess I need to be more thankful for who I am and pray that God will show me the areas that I need to change. In the meantime, I'll have to think of some way to nicely let Liz know that she's really bugging me!

Thursday, October 24 (confrontation!)

Well, I did the deed. The other day, I told Liz that I didn't mind sharing stuff with her, but that I'd appreciate if she'd ask first. She just kind of looked blankly at me and said, "Sure, whatever." And since then, I haven't really noticed anything missing, so maybe she was actually listening. Then I got up the nerve to ask her about Jordan yesterday. He'd been noticeably absent for the last few days.

"Oh, we broke up," she said lightly as if it didn't even matter.

"Again?"

She rolled her eyes at me then flopped onto her bed.

"Well, maybe it's for the best." Okay, I should've known better than to express an opinion about someone else's dating life. After all, I've had lots of bad experiences with my own friends (and they actually like me!).

She narrowed her eyes at me. "How would you know?"

"Oh, I don't know. But it didn't seem like that relationship was doing you much good."

She made a growling sound, then sat up straight and glared at me. "And what makes you an expert on relationships, Miss Goody Two-Shoes?"

Well, I'm really getting tired of this "Miss Goody Two-Shoes" business, but I tried to ignore it. "I'm not saying I'm an expert, but it's not too difficult to see when something's not good for someone. I mean, if someone's taking drugs and it's wrecking her life, it doesn't take a genius to observe it. Or if someone's in a relationship that makes her act like a witch—" Oops, but it was too late.

"You think I act like a witch?" her voice raised itself a notch.

"Well, I don't think Jordan brings out the best in you."

"And what makes you such an expert on what's the best in me?"

"All I'm saying is you don't seem all that happy when you and Jordan are together. And I don't think he's the most dependable kind of guy—I mean, remember what happened with Rachel—?"

She pressed her hands over her ears and made a loud groan. "Sometimes you sound just like my moronic mother!"

Gulp. How do you respond to something like that? "Sorry," I said quietly, "but you asked."

"Well, have you ever considered the possibility that it might be you who's making me act like a witch? Assuming that I even am! What with your little Miss Perfect ways and your Sunday school smiles! Crud, you could drive anyone over the edge."

Ouch! Still, I considered her words. "Do you really mean that?"

"Yes! Probably the only reason I've lasted this long with you was because I kept holding out that Jordan and I would be moving in together before too long." She punched her pillow. "And now that's not very likely!"

"Do you want to see if we can get switched?" I asked, and I have to admit that my feelings were pretty hurt just then. I mean, here I thought I was the one doing all the putting up with, and then she unloads on me that I'm the one who's the real pain in the behind (well, at least in her opinion).

"I've already looked into it, and right now there's nothing available. But don't worry, I'm first on the waiting list."

"Oh." I pretended to busy myself with straightening up my desk, my back to her, but tears of anger mixed with humiliation burned in my eyes. And no way did I want her to see them.

"So, did I hurt your feelings?" But the way she asked this sounded slightly taunting, like maybe she hoped she had.

I turned around and faced her. "Yeah, to be honest, you did. Are you happy now?"

She pressed her lips together but said nothing.

"Look, Liz, this hasn't been a lot of fun for me either.

I've wanted to switch roommates a lot of times, but then I kept thinking maybe there was a reason for this—"

"Like maybe you could save me?" Her eyes had that hard, flinty look.

"Nooo, not exactly. But maybe I could become your friend."

She looked down at her lap for a moment, then spoke in a low voice that was laced with an emotion I still can't quite put my finger on. But my best guess is that it was hostility mixed with desperation. "Sorry, but you don't have what it takes to be my friend."

"How do you know that?" I sat down on my bed now, praying silently that God would somehow break through Liz's hard shell.

"Because I've known people like you. Yeah, you say you want to be my friend, but all you really want is for me to become just like you—plain, boring, vanilla, white-bread... You don't have the slightest interest in knowing, not to mention accepting, who I really am. If you knew who I really was—man, you'd be so freaked out and appalled that you'd probably run home, crying to Mommy and Daddy."

Well, now that one got to me, and I suppose it pushed me into my old sarcastic mode—not something I'm terribly proud of. "So who are you really, Liz? A serial murderer? Drug pusher? Or do you sacrifice children on the devil's altar? What exactly is it that I'd find so appalling about you?"

"For starters I am a woman who doesn't need your

God. I can think for myself, and I can stand on my own two feet. I can have sex with any guy I like, and I can get wasted whenever I feel the urge. I can break the rules and still come out on top. I'm everything you're not, Caitlin, and I know that you hate me for it."

I tried not to blink or register any reaction. "You do drugs too?"

For some reason, although I was perfectly serious, this made her laugh. "Well, I tried them in high school. But I didn't like the way I felt afterward and decided it wasn't my thing. Why do you ask?"

"I don't know. Just curious."

"So you see, Little Goody Two-Shoes, we can never be friends."

"Only because you're not willing to give it a try. I think the truth is you're afraid of me because I make you uncomfortable."

"Oh, sure, you bet." She crossed her legs and acted like she was suppressing a big laugh.

"Then why do you work so hard keeping me at arm's length all the time? Why do you go out of your way to be so mean, to shove me away from you? What are you afraid of anyway?"

"I'm not afraid of anything."

"Oh, I think you are. And as sad as it seems to me, I think you're afraid of God."

"See, I knew it would come down to this. Sooner or later you people always bring everything back to

God. God this, God that. Blah, blah, blah. I'm sick of it!"

"You wouldn't react so strongly if you weren't afraid." I looked evenly at her. "And you wouldn't reject my friendship if you weren't attempting to reject God."

"So you're saying that you can only offer me your friendship if I take your God right along with you?"

I thought about that for a moment. I considered how Jesus had reached out to people—fishermen and tax collectors and harlots. Didn't He simply invite them to come along with Him, to see what developed along the way? But then He's Jesus and I'm me. Still, I thought it might be worth a try. "No, I'm just offering my friendship to you, Liz, plain and simple. That's all. What you do with my offer is entirely up to you."

"So are you saying that should I become your friend, you wouldn't drag me off to your church or preach at me or even criticize me for the way I live?"

"Even if I wanted to, I couldn't drag you to church. And hopefully I wouldn't preach at you, although I've been known to do it from time to time. Still, it's a habit I've been trying to break." I glanced at her and thought I noticed her face soften a little. "And as far as criticizing, well, sometimes that's just what friends do, isn't it? I mean, when you really care about someone and you see them doing something harmful or stupid, don't you want to tell them?"

"And what if I think going to church is harmful or stupid for you?"

"Well, I guess I'd be interested to hear your opinions—if we were friends, that is."

She seemed to be considering all this, and I thought perhaps progress had actually been made.

"Sooo." She looked at me with a little spark in her eye. "What if I said I wanted us to be friends and then invited you to go out with me for a few drinks?"

"I'd have to ask what kind of drinks."

"You know what I mean. A brewsky or two. Would you do it?"

"First of all, I'm only eighteen—"

"I can get you a fake ID."

"That's not the point. Besides being legally underage, I have absolutely no desire to drink alcohol."

"How would you even know, Goody Two-Shoes?"

"Because I tried it. Like you said about drugs, I tried drinking in high school and discovered that I felt totally rotten afterward. It doesn't do anything for me. I'd rather get high on God."

She laughed in that hard way. "So if we were friends, what exactly would we do together? Have little tea parties? Bake cookies? Play Parcheesi?"

Now I laughed. "I suppose we'd just hang out and talk, and hopefully be there for each other. Don't you know what friends do?"

Her eyes flashed now, and I knew I'd gone one step too far. She stood up. "My friends know how to have a good time. They know how to party and enjoy life."

"And so do mine. We just do it in such a way that we still feel great when the party's over."

Well, that made her really mad, and she stormed out, slamming the door behind her. Still, I think progress was made tonight.

EIGHT

Sunday, October 27 (a brief reprieve)

At last, I can honestly say I had a really
good weekend here at school. The day after Liz and I
had our big "friendship" talk (which was really getting
to me, especially considering that I don't exactly have
a plethora of friends here at college), Kim invited me
to join her and some others for the homecoming festivities this weekend. And it was really fun! I got to know
Kim and her roommate Lindsey better, as well as a
bunch of other kids from the fellowship group. It makes
me look forward to not having a night class next
semester.

Anyway, we went to the game and the dance and
just had a good time hanging out as a group. Amazingly,
there hasn't been much pairing off yet, although I did
notice Stephen around Lindsey a lot. But I really like
that these guys seem happy to just hang out as a group.

And they're planning all sorts of fun stuff for this year—things to look forward to.

I felt a little bad about Liz this weekend because she seemed really bummed and lonely. I even invited her to join our group for the homecoming events. Of course, she just laughed that one off. "Yeah, sure, and maybe I'll bring along a Bible to the football game too," she sniped as I bundled up.

"Are you going to do anything?" I asked with my hand on the door.

"Don't worry." She rolled her eyes. "I think this will be my weekend to finally hit the books."

I tried not to look too surprised. "Well, happy studying then." Fortunately I missed most of her last derogatory comment as I slipped out the door. Poor Liz.

Unfortunately for her, the weekend only got worse. I had already suspected that Rachel and Jordan were seeing each other again since I noticed them together outside the dorm last week. But I wasn't sure if Liz knew, or if she did, maybe she just didn't care. I did know this, however: I didn't plan on being the one to spill the beans to her. As it turned out, I didn't need to. And this is where the story gets really good (or bad, depending on how you look at it).

This afternoon after I'd been to church then out for burgers with Kim and some of the other girls, we walked into the dorm lobby just in time to see Liz and Rachel really getting into it. Apparently Liz had gone up to Rachel's room to borrow a CD but then discovered

Jordan there. And let's just say the fur did fly!

I later learned that the three of them had come downstairs, yelling and cussing all the way and even gathering a small audience. Then Jordan somehow slipped out the front door while Rachel and Liz were still arguing. Just as Kim and Lindsey and I walked in, the two girls were actually getting physical. Rachel had Liz by the hair, and they were both swinging and clawing and screaming, and it was really ugly!

I felt bad for Liz but didn't quite know what to do, and everyone else was just standing around and watching. Kim didn't waste a moment as she immediately screamed at them to stop. Then I decided to jump in and see if I could break them apart. I grabbed hold of Rachel's sweatshirt, trying to pull her away from Liz (who actually appeared to be getting the worst of it). Thankfully, Lindsey (a sturdy girl) jumped in to help me and then Kim actually started pulling on Liz. I can't imagine what the five of us must've looked like. Talk about a catfight.

Finally we got the two girls apart and everyone was breathing hard. You could almost feel the adrenaline in the air. Rachel had a bright red scratch on her cheek and a clump of Liz's dark hair in her hand. Both girls actually looked like they were on the verge of tears. At this point I honestly didn't know what to do, but fortunately Kim is one of those take-charge kinds of people.

"What are you two trying to do?" she demanded. "Kill each other?"

Liz narrowed her eyes. "It's her fault!"

I felt Rachel jerk and Lindsey and I both tightened our grips on her arms. "Take it easy," I said in what I hoped was a calm voice. By now I'd already been praying silently, pleading with God to do something miraculous. "Fighting isn't going to solve anything."

Rachel turned and looked at me with angry blue eyes. "Then why don't you tell your freaked-out room- mate to keep her hands off me?"

"Why don't you keep your hands off my boyfriend?" demanded Liz. And suddenly both girls were yelling and cussing all over again.

"You know this isn't really our problem," said Kim loudly. "Maybe we should just let you two go at it, so you can really mess each other up."

I glanced uneasily at Kim. This didn't seem like a very good solution to me. Despite my problems with Liz, I do have some protective feelings toward her. And I even hoped we'd been making some progress toward friendship.

"Fine," snapped Rachel holding up her fist of hair, "I'd be happy to pull it all out!"

"I thought you guys were friends," I said. "Are you really going to let a guy come between you like this?"

"Friends?" Rachel spat out the word. "Liz isn't any- body's friend." She looked at me. "You should know that as well as anyone, Caitlin! Just look at the way she treats you!"

I glanced over at Liz and noticed how bright her dark eyes looked—was it possible that she was really about to cry? I'd never seen her shed a single tear.

"You two just need to chill," said Lindsey. "Why don't we walk you up to your rooms?" Then without allowing time for a response, she and Kim began to escort Rachel toward the elevator. I stayed behind with Liz, not exactly sure of what I should do.

"Are you okay?" I asked dumbly, knowing as soon as the words were out that I was setting myself up for a snide comeback. But she didn't say anything. By now the bystanders had thinned out, but I waited a few minutes before I suggested we go up to our room.

We walked silently up the stairs, the sounds of our footsteps echoing through the stairwell. Liz's were slow and flat sounding, unlike her usual sharp, no-nonsense steps. I prayed that God would give me the right things to say, but had no idea what that would be.

Finally we were in our room, and I asked Liz if she wanted me to fix her a cup of cocoa. She sat down on her bed and nodded without speaking. I kept praying silently as I moved about mixing the packages of cocoa with water, then waiting for the microwave to heat them.

"Here," I handed her the cup then sat down on my bed with mine. "If you want to talk, I'm willing to listen. But I'll understand if you don't."

She took several sips without speaking.

"I know you don't think I have what it takes to be your friend, Liz. And I know you don't like how God is so important to me. But I want you to know that I'm here for you. Even if you don't want to be a friend to me, I'd like to be a friend to you."

But still she said nothing. And usually it really bugs me when someone won't talk or respond, but for some reason it didn't this time. I just got out my books and started doing homework. Then after a while I slipped in a CD, a quiet one, and let it play softly. The next time I looked over to check on Liz, she was fast asleep.

Now it's almost ten and she's still sleeping. I feel really sorry for her, but I don't know if there's anything I can do. Other than keep praying for her, of course. But I know that ultimately she's the one who has to make some changes in her life. And I really think God is trying to get her attention. I just hope she'll listen.

DEAR GOD, I LIFT LIZ UP TO YOU AGAIN. I PRAY THAT YOU WILL USE WHAT HAPPENED TODAY TO BREAK THROUGH HER TOUGH EXTERIOR. SHOW HER THAT SHE NOT ONLY NEEDS YOU, BUT THAT SHE ALSO NEEDS A GOOD FRIEND. AND PLEASE HELP ME TO BE ONE. AMEN.

Friday, November 1

It's been a fairly quiet and uneventful week. A relief, I suppose, after last weekend's little episode with Liz. She's been pretty subdued, and actually seems to be more involved in her studies. But I don't feel we've made any actual progress in the friendship area. After yesterday's conversation with Rachel, I seriously wonder if we ever will.

I ran into Rachel after my last class, and to be honest I was a little frightened. I mean, she was pretty upset last weekend and could've assumed my allegiance was with Liz (although I'm really not taking sides here). At first I pretended not to see her, but it was obvious she was heading straight toward me.

"I've been wanting to talk to you, Caitlin."

"Oh, uh—"

She must've read my expression. "Oh, don't worry; I'm not going to assault you or anything. I just want to talk. Do you have time for a Coke or something?"

I shrugged, still not sure this was a wise thing to do. I couldn't imagine what might happen if Liz spotted us together, but then something about Rachel's expression made me curious. "Okay, I guess I have time."

We ducked into a diner and were barely seated when Rachel started spilling her guts. First she told me how upset she'd been over the fight on Sunday, how she's never been involved in anything like that before. But how Liz pushed her way too far over this thing with Jordan. Then she said how she'd been friends with Liz since their junior year in high school. Not really best friends, mind you, but pretty good friends.

"For Liz, that is." She paused to sip her drink.

"What do you mean?"

She eyed me. "I think you know what I mean. Liz has, shall we say, a somewhat prickly personality."

I nodded. "She's a bit on the cool side."

"And even though I'm still pretty mad at her and feel fairly certain my friendship with her is finished, I'm a little concerned for her."

"Yeah. So am I."

"And since you're her roommate, I thought maybe I should clue you in to a few things about her."

I felt my brows arch. Although I was curious, I wasn't sure if this was right or not. What if Rachel was trying to turn me against Liz too? Still, I figured I could take the advice with a grain of salt (as my grandma would say).

"Liz grew up in a pretty religious family—"

"No way! You're kidding!"

She nodded. "Yep. You'd never know it, would you?"

"But she seems so anti—"

"Oh, yeah, she ditched the whole church thing back in high school." Rachel glanced around then lowered her voice. "I think something bad happened to her, something to do with her church, and it just really turned her against the whole religion scene." She looked at me. "Now I know you're pretty into church and stuff, and I don't mean to offend you, but it's not my thing. I just think that something bad went down with Liz, you know?"

"Did she ever mention anything specific?"

"No. Whatever it was happened before we became friends. We didn't start hanging together until the end of our junior year." Rachel laughed. "I was actually pretty wild compared to her—I mean, before she started changing, that is. We didn't really have much in common before that."

I felt like my head was spinning as I attempted to take it all in. "But why are you telling me this?"

"I guess because, despite what happened last week, I still care about her. Even though she tries to act all cool and unaffected, she really feels things deeply, and this stuff with Jordan and me is probably hitting her a lot harder than it appears..."

"And?"

"And I'm sort of worried that she might do something, you know...something stupid."

Suddenly I remembered Jewel Garcia. "Are you suggesting that she might—" But I couldn't even bring myself to say it.

Rachel nodded solemnly. "I've been around her at other times when she's been pretty depressed, and she's talked about how meaningless life is and how it's not worth the effort and all kinds of dark stuff like that." She sighed. "And, hey, I might not be religious or anything, but I do believe in God or some kind of Supreme Being, and I think there must be some sort of purpose in life, enough anyway that would keep me from giving up on it altogether."

"But you think Liz might."

"I just don't know for sure. You know, I've heard that some people just talk about it but never really do it."

"Yeah, well some people actually do." I felt a surge of

irritated anger rising up in me just then. Like, how did I get pulled into something like this again? I mean, I came here to go to school, then got this whacked-out room-mate with all these issues, and now I have to contend with the possibility that she might actually try to do herself in. Sheesh, what's up with this anyway? Okay, okay, I know I'm sounding pretty self-centered and insensitive, but that's how I felt. Then I told Rachel a little about Jewel and how her breakup with her boyfriend pushed her over the edge.

"She didn't die right off," I continued in what I know must've sounded like an unemotional voice. "She suffered brain damage from the bullet wound but slowly started recovering. We actually thought she was going to make it, but then she started hemorrhaging and finally went into a coma and died."

Rachel shook her head. "I'm sorry."

I looked into her eyes and felt a little surprised at the sincere concern I saw there. "Yeah, me too. Jewel hadn't been a really close friend before the—uh, suicide attempt, but afterward I spent a lot of time visiting her in the hospital. And I really prayed for her to get well..."

"But she didn't."

I thought about that. "Actually, she did. I believe that people are made completely whole and well in heaven."

A somewhat skeptical look darkened her face. "Are you saying you actually believe that someone who <u>shoots</u>

herself will go to heaven—if there is a heaven, that is?"

"I believe it with my whole heart. Jewel became a Christian in the hospital, and I have no doubt that she's in heaven right now."

"Well, you have a lot of faith."

"Actually, I only had a little bit of faith—to start with anyway."

"What do you mean?"

"When I first decided to give my life to God, I wasn't that sure I could even do it. I mean, I had a tiny bit of faith, but that was all. Then after I made the decision, it's like God suddenly gave me more faith. He's the one who gives us the faith to follow Him. We just have to choose to accept it."

"Wow, I've never heard anything like that."

Now I'm sure my face must've lit up then, and suddenly Rachel was holding up both hands. "Slow down, church girl, this doesn't mean I'm interested," she said quickly. "I don't want you to get your hopes up, thinking you can save me or anything."

I laughed. "It's all right. I know I can't save anyone. And don't worry, I won't start following you around or knocking you over the head with my Bible or anything."

She sighed. "Good. You had me worried there."

"But I might be praying for you."

She smiled. "Well, that's okay. I could probably use some prayers. Just don't expect any big response on my part."

I thought about my roommate. "So do you have any suggestions about Liz?"

"I really don't know what to tell you." She grinned. "I'm sure you're already praying for her."

"Yeah, but it doesn't look as if that's helping much." I kind of wished I hadn't said that, but it was honest and how I felt.

"I guess just watch out for any bad signs. And try to be her friend."

I groaned. "Oh, yeah, that's easy enough."

"I know. Jordan and I can't quite figure that one either. It's not easy being her friend. And really, Jordan's a decent guy, but Liz just scares him off. She scares me a little too."

"To be perfectly honest, she scares me too, but I believe God is bigger, and for some reason He's put me in her life. So I guess I'll just have to hang in there—at least for now."

And even as I'm sitting here now, I must admit the idea of a possibly suicidal roommate really freaks me out. And as much as I'm trying to lean on God, I feel uncertain. I think I may give my uncle Tony a call tomorrow. Even though I'm not living at home, I still consider him to be my pastor. Hopefully, he'll have some good insight or advice. In the meantime, I'll really be praying hard for Liz. In fact, I think I'll e-mail everyone I know and ask them to pray specifically for her. And who knows what God might do!

DEAR GOD, PLEASE KEEP YOUR HAND ON LIZ. YOU
ALONE KNOW WHAT'S GOING ON INSIDE HER HEAD
AND HEART RIGHT NOW. PLEASE KEEP HER SAFE
AND HELP HER TO KNOW HOW MUCH YOU LOVE HER.
AND HELP ME TO LOVE HER TOO. AMEN.

NINE

Despite Rachel's warning about Liz,
we made it through the weekend intact. And I haven't
seen any sign of firearms, sleeping pills, or nooses hanging
around. Okay, I know I must sound awfully cynical
(maybe Liz is wearing off on me), but I guess it's the
only way I can get through this stuff right now. And it's
not that I don't take Rachel's concerns seriously—I
most definitely do! I just don't want to dwell on it too
much. Instead I try to pray and keep my eyes wide
open.

But speaking of Rachel, it hits me as slightly ironic
that I suddenly feel closer to her (after one conversation) than I've ever felt with Liz. Of course, I wouldn't
want Liz to know this because I'm certain that despite
her cool demeanor she must still be totally furious at
both Rachel and Jordan. Yet she hasn't said a word

about that whole thing. And she spent most of the weekend working on a psychology paper. I'm thinking perhaps she's throwing herself into her studies to distract herself from the pain in her life. Hey, it's better than doing nothing, and it's a whole lot better than killing yourself!

Okay, enough of that. Here's something that's got me thinking. A bunch of us took a bike ride on Saturday. (What a totally beautiful day it was with sunshine and crisp autumn air and colorful leaves everywhere!) And I noticed that Bryce seemed to be hanging out with me a lot, or maybe it's just because we wanted to go faster than the others. But when we finished our ride and all went out for pizza, he sat next to me, and eventually he told me that he and his girlfriend had broken up last week.

"Oh, I'm sorry," I said without really thinking. (Since that's pretty much the expected thing to say.)

"Yeah, I guess I should've seen it coming though."

"Why's that?" I sipped my soda and glanced at Stephen and Lindsey, across the table. They were engaged in what seemed a very interesting discussion over whether women should be allowed to become pastors or not. But then I turned my attention back to Bryce.

"Oh, you know how it goes." His voice sounded glum. "The e-mails were decreasing, and it was just a feeling I was getting, like something was about to die or maybe already had..."

"So did she break it off with you?" Now even as I asked this, I wondered why I was continuing this conversation when it actually felt a little more personal than I was willing to get into. I mean, I like Bryce just fine, but a tiny red flag went up inside of me, like a warning signal that maybe I shouldn't go here. Still, he's the one who brought all this stuff up, and maybe he just needed a good friend to talk with.

"It was mutual. I think we both knew it was time to end."

"Even so, it must be kind of hard, letting the relationship go."

"Yeah, it makes me sorta sad. We'd been together for a long time." He stirred the ice around with his straw.

Suddenly Stephen leaned over. "Hey, are you getting all gloomy over Amy again?"

Bryce smiled a half smile. "No, not really. But it takes some adjusting."

Stephen winked at me. "Well, I'm sure Caitlin can help you with the transition period."

Now for whatever reason, this made me mad. I knew Stephen was only joking, but the idea that Bryce was suddenly not as "safe" as when we'd first become friends made me feel uncomfortable and slightly irritated. Suddenly I felt like maybe I should say something about my nondating commitment. Still, it seemed kind of ridiculous to get up on my soapbox and tell everyone at the table about my private and personal convictions. Besides, as all my old friends will attest, I've been there and done that. And most of the time it just backfires right in my face.

Not only that, but how would that make Bryce feel? Would he think I'd assumed he was coming on to me when all he wanted was a friend to listen to him? Or would he think I was judging him for having been involved with a girlfriend? Whatever the ramifications, I simply did <u>not</u> want to go there. And so, for a refreshing change, I kept my mouth shut.

I guess if the time comes or the need arises, I can always let Bryce know where I stand—privately, that is. Until then I hope we can just be good friends. But since I'm still human, I must admit that I don't mind the idea of Bryce being attracted to me. I mean, he's a great guy who really loves God (and he's good looking too!). I'd be less than honest to pretend that I don't think it's nice to think he's interested in me. Still, I know I need to maintain my boundaries. And the truth is, I'd still be more interested in Josh than anyone. Blush!

But speaking of Josh, I'm feeling a little slighted since his e-mails have been decreasing too. In fact, when Bryce said that about Amy, I got a little chill thinking that perhaps Josh and I may have reached a similar fork in the road. Oh, I know Josh and I don't have anything serious going on. We both know that. But I know that underneath everything (and here's gut-level honest!), I'm kind of hoping we'll end up together eventually. And I don't think there's anything really wrong with that. That is, unless God has other plans. And I suppose that's a distinct possibility. But it's a possibility I'd rather not think about. That's probably why I usually try to keep these thoughts at bay, since they usually only serve to confuse and frustrate me.

DEAR GOD, ONCE AGAIN, I NEED TO HAND MY FUTURE OVER TO YOU. I CONFESS THAT TOO OFTEN I ALLOW MYSELF (EVEN IF ONLY FOR A FLEETING MOMENT) TO THINK ABOUT JOSH. YOU KNOW MY FEELINGS FOR HIM. (I CAN'T HIDE ANY-THING FROM YOU.) AND IF THEY'RE WRONG, PLEASE HELP ME TO DEAL WITH THEM IN THE RIGHT WAY. MOSTLY I JUST WANT YOU TO KNOW THAT I TRUST YOU WITH EVERYTHING—EVEN JOSH. I LOVE YOU, LORD! AMEN.

Friday, November 8 (ARRRRGHH!!!!)

Disaster, disaster, disaster. No, my roommate hasn't shot herself. But let me tell you, it's a good thing I didn't have a gun in _my_ hands this evening, because I just might've shot her myself! Okay, _not really_! Good grief, I would never do that. Still, I was seriously mad! Furious even! Actually I'm still pretty angry.

This is what happened. I went with Kim and Lindsey to get deli sandwiches for dinner tonight. Then, worn out from what felt like a very long week, I came home to just kick back and relax. But when I walked into my room, I found Liz sitting at _my_ desk—reading _my_ diary!!!

"What are you doing?" I demand, tossing my backpack onto my bed and planting my hands on my hips in an I'm-very-angry pose.

But she doesn't even budge, just looks up at me with dark and narrowed eyes, like she wants to kill me. Suddenly I wonder how far she'd gotten in it. How much has she read that is about her? I know I've ranted about her quite a bit—especially since she tends to be my greatest cross to bear of late.

"Give it to me!" I stick out my hand with a look on my face that I hope adequately conveys my outrage.

She closes it, and from the best I can tell, she's only read about twenty pages or so. (More than enough to read about herself and my opinions of her.) "You can really get to know someone by reading her diary," she says as she hands it back to me, still scowling.

"I cannot believe you'd stoop so low as to read someone else's diary! What in the world is wrong with you, Liz?"

"Why don't you read it for yourself. It seems you have me all figured out in there."

"I will never have you figured out!" I stuff my diary into my backpack, promising myself never to leave it out of my sight again. Even my own little brother had never dared to step over this line! And it's not like I'd left it out in the open either. I had put it where I sometimes do, in the second drawer, tucked inconspicuously beneath a spiral notebook.

"Oh, I thought you had everyone and everything figured out. You and that amazing God of yours." Her tone of voice was acidic, poisonous, lethal even.

"What I want to know is, do you go pawing through my things all the time or were you just particularly bored this evening?"

"The truth is, you really don't interest me that much, Caitlin. I was simply looking for some printer paper. I'm all out."

I reach over to my printer where a small stack of paper is clearly visible, grab a handful, and thrust it toward her. "Here, I guess you didn't see this."

"As it turns out, I'm glad I read your diary. It confirms that I was right."

"Right about what?"

"You." Then she walks over to her side of the room, sits on her bed, casually crosses her legs, and looks up at me with what seems like totally unveiled hatred. In that moment, I feel almost as if I'm looking into the devil's eyes. To say it is unsettling is a total understatement.

I sink onto my bed (with rubbery knees) and just look at her. Is this a conversation worth having, or would I be better off to simply run the other way? I knew that Kim and Lindsey would gladly put me up for the night, or longer, since they've both seriously concerned that I'm living with a raving maniac. Kim actually thinks Liz is demon possessed. (Her home church is really into that stuff.) But the truth is, tonight I wondered if Kim might actually be on to something. And so I sit here and pray silently, begging God to tell me what to do—and to protect me.

"What do you want from me?" I finally ask, not even sure why I said this. Maybe it was just a God thing.

"Nothing."

"Then why are you doing this? Why would you read my diary? Do you not understand that a diary is extremely personal?"

"Well, I'll admit it was wrong. But then we know that I'm the bad girl here, don't we? You make that perfectly clear in your diary. Oh, poor little Caitlin, the darling saint who has to room with the evil Liz. It's all there in black and white."

I just shake my head. How do you respond to something like this?

"And the fact is, I'm really not all that surprised by what I read. You're exactly who I thought you were—a freaked-out religious hypocrite!"

Now I am really wondering what I'd written about her. I mean, it's not as if I go back and reread all the stuff I write. A diary is supposed to be a place where you can freely express your feelings—good and bad—without the fear that someone will be looking over your shoulder. That's why I made sure I wrote again tonight. Kind of like getting right back onto the horse that just threw you off. I was worried that if I didn't write tonight, I might be too afraid to write later. And I'm not willing to give Liz that victory. I will continue to express myself honestly and openly. I'll just make sure I don't ever leave this where she or anyone else can get hold of it! But back to our conversation.

"I don't know how you can call me a hypocrite," I tell her. "What I write in my diary is the truth—for me anyway—it's how I feel at the time. Right or wrong, it's the stuff I'm going through. How can you judge that as hypocritical?"

"You don't think it's hypocritical for someone to go around acting like she's all sweetness and light, Goody Two-Shoes, Pollyanna—and then to write nasty and vicious things about someone else in her diary?"

"Look, Liz, maybe you don't quite understand the purpose of a diary—"

"Don't get on your high horse with me!"

"A diary isn't meant to be read by anyone except the author! Those thoughts are private and personal. I've never said I was perfect. Believe it or not, things can get to me. You get to me. And sometimes I just need a place—what I previously considered a safe place—to relieve some of that pressure."

She rolls her eyes. "Whatever."

"You're not even sorry, are you?"

"Why should I be sorry? You're the one always pretending to be perfect. I'm only living according to my own personal standards."

"You mean you think it's okay to get into my things? Is that your standards?"

She shrugs.

Well, this is really feeling like way too much for me, and I am about ready to stomp right out of here, but then I remember something that Tony had said last week when I called and told him a little about my situation with Liz. "Sometimes when a person really goes out of their way to push you away or hurt you, it's a sign that they're a lot closer than you think to making a real breakthrough. God may be using you a lot more than you realize right now."

And suddenly I know if God is going to use me, I'd have to take the high road. And so after taking a deep breath and slowly exhaling I say. "You know, Liz, I'm sorry that the things I wrote hurt you—"

"They didn't hurt—"

"Just let me finish, okay?" I stand up. "Really, I'm sorry. I hadn't meant to hurt you. I was only venting some of my frustrations. I do that a lot in my diary. In fact, you should try it. It's a great way to work some things out. Anyway, I know you probably don't even care, but I forgive you for trespassing into my space."

"You're right!" she snaps. "I could care less." Then she jumps up and storms out without even putting her coat on.

I was kind of relieved (since I thought I'd be the one who had to evacuate the premises tonight). But at the same time I felt a little worried for her. She seems so hopeless and desperate right now. And suddenly I have the feeling that this is all between her and God. Like she's engaged in this big battle with Him. I know that sounds slightly melodramatic, but it's how it feels to me.

Anyway, I've got everyone I know praying for her, and I've been putting in overtime myself on her behalf. I just hope that something happens soon, because the truth is,

I'm feeling a little worn down by all this. Still, I know we're not supposed to get weary of doing what God wants us to do because when the time is right it'll all work out. I only hope that time is soon!

TEN

Tuesday, November 12 (life is so daily)

I don't remember anyone ever warning me
that life is <u>supposed</u> to be hard. I guess I should know this
by now, but there's this little place inside me that still
has this expectation that life should be easy or fun or
at the least somewhat pleasant. Now I'm not saying that
my life is totally miserable. But it seems that I'm never
completely free of problems (or "challenges," depending on
your frame of mind at the time). And I know that these
struggles should make me stronger and build up my character and that I should be thankful for them (or greet
them like friends as the first chapter of James so
clearly says). But sometimes I just want to take a little
vacation from it all. You know, cruise off to the Island of
Bliss and flop down on a warm sunny beach and totally
forget about everything else.

Liz has been giving me the silent treatment lately,

which is perfectly fine with me since I'm not sure I have
anything to say to her right now anyway. I keep praying,
as much for me as for her, since I often feel as if I'm
near the end of my rope, and I worry that I'll do something stupid like explode at her and say all kinds of
horrible things.

I pray for self-control a lot these days. But sometimes
it feels like I'm this fatigued soldier just trudging along,
shoving one weary foot in front of the other, wondering
when this battle will end. If it is a battle, that is,
because sometimes I think maybe I'm putting myself in
harm's way for absolutely no good reason. Like why don't
I just pack it all up and find a new place to live? Maybe I
could camp out in the hallway until something better
turned up.

I'll bet people would feel sorry for me parked out
there since by now almost everyone in the dorm knows Liz
is a bit difficult to live with. Of course, this also
decreases my chances of getting someone to switch with
me (because who'd want to room with her?). However, I've
heard that things change during winter break, and
since Liz is first on the waiting list, I'm thinking my
chances of having a new roommate by January are
pretty good.

But it's not just the Liz dilemma that's got me down.
I'll admit that I'm feeling a little blue as a result of not
hearing from Josh for a couple of weeks now. And I don't
really want to e-mail him again until he responds to my
last e-mail—I don't want to seem pushy or eager.

Because I know he's busy. But even when I'm busy, I still take time to communicate with my friends. Of course, as they all remind me, it's easy for me since I love to write. And not everyone is like that. So I probably just need to be more patient.

On the brighter side, Beanie called me last night. At first she sounded pretty glum (not unlike me), but I tried to cheer her up, lest we both fall into the pity-party trap, which I frankly did not need! Anyway, after about twenty minutes we were both feeling much better. Apparently, she and Jenny had gotten into a little spat. About—guess what? A boy! Ha! I tried not to overreact about this. I didn't give any lectures or sermons or "I told you so's." Instead I just listened as Beanie told me all about Danny (the drummer in the Christian rock band that goes to their college). Apparently, Danny (the same boy Jenny's had a slight crush on since last spring when we went up there to visit the school) has taken an interest in Beanie.

"At first I was just really flattered," Beanie explained. "And I joked with him and didn't take it too seriously. To be honest, I thought he might've been just fooling around with me. I mean, to think a guy like that would be more interested in me than Jenny is so—"

"Beanie!" I cut her off. "You're always running yourself down! Don't you know what a great person you are? I totally love Jenny and she's terrific, but so are you. And you guys are completely different...there's not even a way to compare you. You're like apples and oranges."

"Thanks, Cate." I could hear the smile creeping back into her voice. "This whole thing would've been no big deal if Jenny hadn't been so psyched over Danny. I mean, she talks about him all the time, and she goes to all his performances, and I actually think if she'd just played a little more hard to get, he might've gotten interested."

I laughed. "Like you did."

"I wasn't playing hard to get!"

"I know, I know. I just mean it probably seemed like that to him."

"Anyway, I told Jenny I was absolutely not interested in him. But she was pretty mad anyway. Not at me exactly, but just the whole situation. And she started acting pretty chilly toward me, and then she'd toss out these little snide comments..."

"You know she doesn't mean it, Beanie. She's just hurting."

"I know, but it hurts my feelings. Especially coming from Jenny. She even got on me about eating a donut, telling me I was already too fat and—"

"Beanie!" I cut her off again. "You are NOT fat. Sure, you have a different build than Jenny..." I paused, remembering Jenny's struggle with anorexia last fall. "She's still eating okay, isn't she?"

"Yeah, I think so. But she's been so bummed about Danny that it worries me a little."

"I suppose something like this might make her back-slide though."

"Yeah, and then I did something really stupid, Caitlin."

"What?"

She sighed. "Well, Danny had left a message for me on our answering machine yesterday, which naturally Jenny listened to, before I had a chance to hear it and erase it. And when I got home she sniped at me and then said I better check my messages. So when I heard his message, I grabbed up the phone and called him back— just to spite Jenny—and then I went out and met him for coffee."

"Oh, Beanie." I hadn't wanted to show my disapproval, but it was too late.

"I know, I know. It was totally lame. I mean, I don't even like him—not like that anyway. He's a nice enough guy though."

"So I can imagine how things are between you and Jenny now."

"Yeah. What should I do?"

"What do you want to do?"

"I want to straighten everything out with her. I'm not really interested in Danny..."

"Are you absolutely certain?"

"Well, he's a sweet guy. And it is kind of fun having someone like him interested and paying attention to me." She paused. "But it's not worth hurting Jenny over."

"So what do you want to do then?"

"I already told Danny I was only interested in being friends with him."

"How did he respond to that?"

"Pretty well, actually. He seemed kind of relieved. He said he wasn't looking for any serious romance either, but that he liked me and wanted to get to know me better—as friends."

"That's great."

"Well, not exactly—not when you consider Jenny's feelings."

"Yeah, good point."

"So, should I tell Danny I can't be his friend because of Jenny?"

"Have you told Jenny any of this?"

"No."

"I think you should sit down and have a good heart-to-heart with her and explain the whole thing just like you've explained it to me."

"Yeah, you're probably right."

"And if it's true that you're only going to be friends with Danny, why not include Jenny in the friendship too. Just encourage her not to put any pressure on him. It sounds as if he's only looking for friendship anyway."

"Yeah, that makes sense."

"And let Jenny know that her friendship is more important to you than Danny's is."

"Maybe I'll tell her that I'll totally drop him if she wants me to."

"Are you really willing to do that?"

"I think I am, now that I've thought about it a little."

"Cool. I think she'll appreciate that."

Beanie sighed happily. "Hey, I feel much better now. So how's your life going these days?"

I briefly (very briefly) filled her in on the latest trials with Liz. Beanie's been faithfully praying for her too.

"Just remember you can't save her, Caitlin."

"I know. Believe me, I know."

"And there might come a time when you just need to walk away—for your own sake, that is. Remember how Jesus told His disciples to shake the dust off their feet when people wouldn't listen to them?"

"Yeah. But I keep thinking God must have some reason for putting me with her."

"Well, if anyone can have an impact on someone like this Liz chick, it'll probably be you."

I laughed now. "And why exactly is that?"

"Well, look at how you influenced me. And I was sort of a mess. And don't forget how God used you with Chloe. Talk about what seemed a hopeless case. I honestly didn't think that girl would ever come around."

"Oh, that's just because you didn't know her. She looked really tough on the outside, but underneath it all I could tell she had a really tender heart."

"How's she doing?"

"Really great! She's not afraid to talk to anyone about God. Not only that, but she's started baby-sitting for Steph and Tony's weekly date night."

Beanie laughed. "Following right in my footsteps."

"Funny, isn't it?"

"Well, Steph and Tony will be good for her. That's so cool."

We talked a little more, and by the time we hung up, I was feeling much better. Tonight I'll pray especially for Beanie and Jenny to patch things up. I think Jenny (even more than Beanie) really needs that friendship.

Friday, November 15

The fellowship group is having a pre-Thanksgiving party tomorrow night. It's potluck and a dress-up affair. And since it feels like I'm living at the North Pole (Liz is so chilly), I asked Kim and Lindsey if I could come up to their room to get ready. They seemed happy to have me, so I'm feeling slightly festive today and glad that I brought a few dressier things to college with me. I almost didn't, but Mom reminded me that there could be some special occasions. Of course, that's back when she thought I might join her old sorority. It's funny how that sorority biz looks better as time goes by. Still, it's too late now.

I finally got an e-mail from Josh. And, would you believe it, he hadn't gotten my last e-mail. He'd been having server trouble and feared that perhaps some of his messages had been lost in the interim. But it was so sweet how he wrote to me, since he felt a little unsure that I'd actually answered his last e-mail (more than two weeks ago). So he was kind of tiptoeing around a bit.

He said he'd understand if I was too busy to keep writing or if I had other things going on in my life (which I suspect he meant as "romantic" interests since he mentioned Bryce's name). Anyway, I assured him (without actually saying it) that I was not too busy and enjoyed staying in touch with him. IOW (in other words) as far as I'm concerned, nothing's changed between us.

Now to be honest, it does worry me (just a little) that it meant so much for me to hear from Josh. Man, I was so totally happy yesterday—walking on a cloud. And I'm thinking that's the way I should be for God—not a silly guy! And I have to admit this is bugging me—a lot! But I'm praying about it and hoping God will show me what's up and if there's anything I need to do about this whole thing. Because I really do want to love God <u>most!</u> And I know that's what He wants from me too. He needs to be first, best, and most in my life.

DEAR GOD, PLEASE FORGIVE ME IF I HAVE IN ANY WAY PUT MY FEELINGS TOWARD JOSH ABOVE MY LOVE FOR YOU. I KNOW IN MY HEART THAT YOU MEAN MORE TO ME THAN ANYTHING. I REALLY BELIEVE THAT. BUT I ALSO KNOW THAT OTHER THINGS IN MY LIFE WILL VIE FOR MY AFFECTIONS. PLEASE HELP ME TO RECOGNIZE IF MY PRIORITIES GET MIXED UP. I WANT TO LOVE YOU MORE THAN ALL ELSE. I WANT TO SERVE YOU WITH MY WHOLE HEART, BUT I NEED YOUR HELP. AMEN.

Sunday, November 17 (good old fun)

Oh, it's been a great weekend. A little like that vacation I wanted to take on the Island of Bliss. I guess God
knows when we need a break. And tonight I feel totally
refreshed—spiritually, emotionally, even physically. The
party last night was a lot of fun. I met a bunch of new
kids, and it really makes me look forward to next semester when I can get more involved in the fellowship group.
As planned, I went to Kim and Lindsey's room. Fortunately
those two are getting along better these days. I think
seeing Rachel and Liz going at it helped them to appreciate each other more. Not only that, they've been much
more compassionate toward my suffering. And although
they're praying for Liz (and Rachel too), they both think I
should switch roommates after fall term ends. I still
don't know for sure.

But anyway, right after my last class, I hauled all my
stuff up to their room. (They'd already suggested I
spend the night there after the party.) And together we
managed to concoct our contributions to the potluck
dinner, using only a microwave and a hot plate. We made
a fruit salad, coleslaw, and the real challenge, "can-
died yams." But all in all our dishes didn't look too bad.
Then we helped each other get ready. I'd taken several
outfits up. (I hoped they would help me decide since I've
never been to a fellowship party here, and I didn't want
to over- or underdress for the occasion.) As it turned out,
they encouraged me to wear the dressiest dress (a mid-

night blue velvet number with glass beads that Steph had given me after she got pregnant with Clayton). But I didn't have the right shoes.

"I've got some that'll be perfect," said Kim.

"But you're so petite," I protested. I'm guessing she's barely five feet tall.

She grinned. "But my feet are size seven and a half."

"You're kidding. That's perfect!"

Then Lindsey insisted on putting up my hair. Somewhat skeptical, I almost said no. But when I saw the hope on her face, I gave in. What difference would it make if I ended up looking like the prom queen or even a clown. This party was just for fun anyway. Then to my surprise, she actually did a great job.

"Oh, Caitlin," gushed Kim when she saw my hair piled high, "you look just like Gwyneth Paltrow at the Oscars. But you're going to need some earrings now. I think I have just the pair."

I stared in amazement at how well Lindsey had arranged the straight blond hair that usually gives me so much trouble when I try to style it in anything outside of the ordinary. "Lindsey, are you sure you're taking the right major? I mean, I'll bet that a really good hairstylist could make more money than a schoolteacher."

She laughed. "You're probably right. But as much as I like styling hair, I can't imagine doing it every day. And as far as teaching goes, it's a good thing I'm not in it for the money."

"Speaking of majors," Kim held up a red silk dress that she'd just finished steaming. "You haven't mentioned yours, Caitlin. I know you want to work with the orphans in Mexico, but what are you taking?"

"Good question. I haven't totally decided. The obvious major is education, maybe early childhood ed. But I really love writing too."

"Lucky for you, you don't have to decide yet," said Lindsey. "I was still torn last year when I had to declare between secondary and elementary ed. But after volunteering in a middle school for a couple of weeks, I had no doubt that I'd rather be with the little kids. I'd completely forgotten how creepy and obnoxious young adolescents can be."

"It's cool that we're all interested in working with kids," said Kim as she put the finishing touches on her makeup.

"Kim, you look gorgeous," I said admiring her exotic-looking Asian beauty.

Lindsey groaned and looked down at her T-shirt and sweatpants. "Now I feel just like Cinderella."

"Poor Lindsey," said Kim. "Don't worry; we'll help you get all glammed up now."

And although Lindsey isn't exactly what you'd call a natural beauty, we (mostly Kim) did manage to get her looking quite stunning. Even she was pleased. "Wow, I really do feel like Cinderella now."

And so we gathered up our food and trekked over to the hall where the festivities were to be held. And as hokey as it sounds, we sang praise songs as we went. I thought for a brief moment at how Liz would scowl and make fun of the three of us. She'd probably call us "prissy little Christian girls who were all dressed up with no place to go." But then I also realized how Liz was probably sitting at home right now, stewing unhappily. Still, I decided I wouldn't allow her to dampen my spirits in any way tonight. And I began to sing with even more gusto, enjoying the clicking sound of Kim's expensive shoes as I danced along the sidewalk with my two new friends.

The only small fly in the ointment (oops, I need to start watching my clichés better—my writing teacher would nab me for this). But anyway, the only black spot on my snowy white evening was that Bryce paid me a little more attention than I wanted. I kept telling myself it was only in a Christian brotherly way, but at the same time I could feel a little alarm going off inside of me. Not that I'm interested in him, mind you, but I just don't want to lead him on either.

As the party was winding to an end, he asked if I needed him to escort me home. But thankfully, I had Kim and Lindsey as excuses to decline his kind offer.

"By the way, Caitlin," he said as I recovered my dish from the potluck. "I'm going home on Wednesday for Thanksgiving. Do you need a ride?"

Well, I knew my parents would gladly come pick me up, but I also knew how much they'd appreciate me getting a ride on my own. And so I agreed. But even as I said the words, I regretted it. But maybe I can use the travel time to somehow, and in a kind way, convey to him my convictions on dating. In a way, my nondating stance makes it much simpler when a situation like this arises. More cut-and-dried, you know? Still, I don't want to hurt him. And it'd be nice if we could remain friends since he has a car and our hometowns are so handily located near each other. It's times like this that I'm really thankful that I made that commitment.

ELEVEN

Friday, November 22 (thankful homecoming)

Oh, it's so great to be home again. And
Thanksgiving was the best ever! Steph and Tony hosted
our family as well as several people from church (who
don't have family around here), and it was the best
time. We stuffed ourselves, then played goofy board
games and watched football and visited. Really laid-
back but very cool.

Today I mostly hung with my family. First I fixed
them breakfast (which completely blew my dad away
since he still thinks I don't get up until noon on non-school
days). After that, Mom and I did some Christmas shopping.
A joke really, since the stores were so packed that we
could barely find anything. Although I did manage to lay
my hands on some sweet little angel ornaments that I
plan to give to my friends.

I think the whole idea of shopping was really just an

excuse for spending time together. I've discovered that living away from home REALLY makes me appreciate my parents—a lot! I can't quite believe it, but I find myself looking up to them more than ever. It's like they've suddenly become so wise and valuable and dependable lately. Or has my perspective changed? Anyway, it's kind of nice to enjoy being around my family.

Tonight we watched a cheesy video that Dad made containing all the highlights of Ben's football games. And it was actually pretty funny. Then we played Pictionary and laughed a lot. I honestly can't remember having an evening like that with my family (where no one got into any squabbles or anything). It felt as if we could've been the model family for a contemporary Norman Rockwell picture. I realize these moments don't come along too often, and so I'm determined to cherish it in my memory for a long time. If nothing else, it should warm my heart when I'm back in my chilly dorm room with Liz.

Speaking of Liz, I'm afraid that she didn't go home for Thanksgiving. I'm not even sure why I think this other than the fact that she didn't seem to be packing up or anything. I asked if she had any plans (I'd been trying to reach out a little more), but she just shrugged and said she wasn't sure yet. So without really thinking, I actually invited her to come home with me. Now, really, I can't imagine what I would've done if she'd agreed (not that she would've, but I think I might have fallen over stone dead if she had). Still, I'm sure my family would've gone out of their way to make her feel at home. They know she's not the easiest girl to get along with. In fact, even today my mom encouraged me to get my room switched before winter term begins.

"It's sweet that you care about this girl, Caitlin," she said tactfully as we ate a quick lunch in the noisy food court at the mall. "But we don't want to see your living situation dragging you down while you're trying to study and keep your grades up. We've all sensed that it's been pretty stressful for you this fall."

And to think they didn't know the half of it! "Yeah, it isn't easy. But I think it's pretty likely that we won't be together after Christmas." I set down my soda and looked at Mom, wondering if she'd really understand. Now, I don't want to sound as if I'm spiritually superior or anything (because I know that's ridiculous), but sometimes it seems like my parents aren't quite as committed or sold out to God as I am. I mean, they still question my goal of serving God full-time with whatever career choice I make. I suspect they think I'm going through a stage or something. So I wasn't sure if Mom would really get what I was about to say. But I decided to try it anyway. "You see, I can't help but think God had a reason for putting me in that room with Liz. As hard and cold as she is, I think she's really looking for answers. And it seems like she has a real problem with church or Christians or religion, and that's probably why she takes it out on me—"

"Takes what out on you?" Mom looked concerned.

I laughed. "Oh, Mom, it's not like she beats me up or

anything. She's just extremely antagonistic toward God. And she has a pretty sharp tongue too." Naturally I didn't mention how Liz might occasionally make an unsaved rapper uncomfortable with her trashed-out vocabulary. "But despite all that, I believe God is working on her. And I think He still wants to use me to..."

"To what?"

I shrugged. "I don't exactly know. Believe me, I realize I can't save her. And I know I'm not an evangelist. But somehow I think all the stuff I've gone through with her this fall is for a purpose. At least I hope it is."

Mom just shook her head.

"And if it makes you feel any better, I've really been praying that God will show me what to do."

Then Mom smiled and patted me on the arm. "I'm sure He will, honey. And even though I do worry about you with that strange girl, I'm still proud of you for handling everything in such a mature way."

Those words meant a lot to me. I know my parents and I still don't see eye to eye about everything. But it's nice to know they respect what I'm doing. I just hope I don't let them down.

Saturday, November 23 (letting go)
Today I hung with Beanie and Jenny (Anna was out of town at an aunt's house), and we had a really good time. Thankfully, Jenny and Beanie have resolved their differences over Danny without any bloodshed or per-

manent disrepair. Apparently, <u>Danny the drummer</u> (they hate when I call him that, but I think it's rather cute) is happy to make their friendship a trio. And all have agreed not to get serious, although I suspect Jenny may still have feelings for him. But then that's what happens when you nurture a crush for an extended period of time. It's an open invitation for heartbreak if you ask me (of course, no one's asking, thank you very much).

Once again I must remind myself of this regarding my own feelings for Josh because despite my image of having it so together (or so my friends think) over this whole "non-dating" thing, I realize that it's still quite possible to have my heart involved whether I'm dating or not. And I'm getting the strong sense that I need to guard my heart more carefully.

Especially after tonight. Okay, just relax now, it's not like Josh and I sneaked out and had a passionate kissing scene again. Thank goodness. What happened is that the youth group in Tony's church was having a little hoedown tonight, and they invited all of us "old-timers" to come. Actually it was a square dance, and you were supposed to come dressed up like someone from out of the Old West. Corny, I know, but fun just the same.

Anyway, I borrowed some stuff from Steph (she used to be into what she calls cowboy dancing—now talk about corny!), but thanks to her I was able to pull together a pretty cute cowgirl outfit, complete with boots and a hat! Jenny and Beanie picked me up. Beanie

looked like a farmer in her bib overalls and a red ban-
danna tied around her neck. And Jenny had on a hilari-
ous pink satin getup that she'd scrounged from her mom.

"She says it's from her urban cowgirl phase,"
explained Jenny with good humor. "I think she actually
wore it during the early eighties."

We three arrived in high spirits and jumped right into
the action. You really don't have to know a whole lot to
be able to square dance since the caller pretty much
tells you what to do. And half the fun is bumbling along
and making a complete fool of yourself anyway. Mostly it
was great to see old friends and act silly and laugh. It's
occurred to me this weekend how I don't laugh nearly as
much as I used to since I started college. This is something I'm hoping will change!

Naturally Chloe was there, since she's pretty involved
in church these days. And she was even decked out in a
pair of old-fashioned blue jeans that came all the way
to the waist and were cinched in with a Western-style
belt.

"Pretty hot," I told her with a wink. "Is this your new
look?"

"Yeah, you bet." She arched an eyebrow and
grinned. "Although I'm sure my parents are hoping..."

"Hey there," Josh said, grabbing my arm. "You ready
to do-si-do with me?"

I laughed and went out with him just in time to do the
Virginia reel. (A dance I still remember from my middle-
school years when I was too shy to even look into my part-

ner's face.) But tonight I looked right into Josh's blue eyes and danced and laughed and really enjoyed myself. When the dance ended, Josh bowed and tipped his cowboy hat, then moseyed on over to Beanie for the next number.

Now, everyone was pretty much dancing with everyone. And since there were more girls than guys, we girls even took turns taking the guys' parts. But I kept hoping that Josh would seek me out for another dance. I tried not to look too obvious as I glanced across the room to see who he was dancing with—sometimes Jenny or Beanie or Andrea or even Chloe. And I couldn't help but notice that he danced with some of them (like Jenny) more than just once. But by the time the evening ended, he had only danced that one single dance with me. And the embarrassing truth is I was feeling slightly irritated and hurt. But at the same time, I kept telling myself that it was senseless and stupid. Why should he feel the need to dance with me at all? And why should I feel so upset that he didn't?

Well, as I'm sitting in my old room writing this, it all feels painfully clear to me. Despite my big talk about remaining "romantically uninvolved," I've let my heart go its own way again, and I need to do something about it. I'm just not sure what that is yet, but I'll pray about it, and hopefully God will show me.

But what's really humbling about this whole thing is that I had planned to have that little talk with Bryce tomorrow. Somehow we never got around to it on

Wednesday. I'm sure it's because I realized I'd need to be riding back to college with him on Sunday and I didn't want to make him (or me) dread the long drive with stilted conversation and uncomfortable silences. Anyway, now I'm feeling just slightly hypocritical. But I'll still try to deal with it—as best I can. Oh, brother. When will I ever learn?

DEAR GOD, I KNOW YOU'RE TRYING TO TEACH ME SOMETHING RIGHT NOW. PLEASE HELP ME TO GET IT. AND SHOW ME HOW TO DEAL WITH MY FEELINGS ABOUT JOSH. AND PLEASE HELP ME TO SPEAK HONESTLY TO BRYCE. OH, GOD, WHAT WOULD I DO WITHOUT YOU? AMEN.

Sunday, November 24

The ride home with Bryce went amazingly well. I waited until we were about halfway to school, and then decided to be completely up front with him.

"I want to tell you something, Bryce," I began, struggling to come up with the right words.

He glanced at me. "Sure, what?"

I could tell by his expression that he was afraid I was going to tell him he had bad breath or something. "Well, it might sound kind of silly, and you may not even care anyway, but it's something I just need to say and get out into the open. Okay?"

He nodded with a puzzled look. "Okay."

"In my junior year in high school, not too long after I accepted the Lord, I made a commitment to God. And some people think it's kind of silly—that's probably why I try not to talk about it too much—but the thing is, I decided to quit dating." Now I couldn't quite read his expression. Maybe it was relief mixed with humor. I'm not totally sure.

"You mean like that book, I Kissed Dating Goodbye?"

"Yeah, sort of. Only it was my own commitment. I made it without reading any book or anything. Just between me and God, y'know?"

He nodded. "Interesting. So does that mean you'll never go out with a guy again—ever?"

I laughed. "I'm not totally sure about the timing. I expect things will change when I'm at an age or a place in life to seriously consider marriage. But until then, I want to avoid getting involved like that."

Then he asked me a lot of questions, and we talked really openly about the whole thing. I told him that I still valued his friendship and hoped this wouldn't change anything.

"It's like my friendships with guys become even more important than when dating was a factor. Maybe it's because there's no pressure there. You just get to enjoy each other's company without always worrying about what comes next."

"Yeah, that sounds cool to me too."

We talked some more, and by the time we reached the city limits, he was saying how that would've been the best thing for him to have done in his relationship with Amy.

"Do you think you'll still be friends with her?" I asked as we pulled onto campus.

"She's already got a new boyfriend." His face looked a little sad.

"Does that hurt?"

He sighed. "Yeah, it does. But I still think that breaking up was for the best."

Then we were in front of my dorm. "I'm glad I could tell you about this." I felt slightly embarrassed. "I mean, it's not like I thought you were dying to ask me out or anything, but it's easier if I just lay my cards on the table."

"Hey, don't kid yourself. I _did_ plan on asking you out. In fact, I would've asked you out today if you hadn't told me about your—your nondating thing."

"So do you think it's silly?"

"Not at all. I think I'll give the whole thing some serious thought myself. I've never been that comfortable with the whole dating thing in the first place. I'm sure that's one reason it was so easy to stay with Amy—all that distance between us just made it easier to deal with. Plus it alleviated the need for me to find someone to date here on campus, like I had an excuse, you know?"

I nodded. I still hadn't told him anything about Josh. Somehow I couldn't see how that would help anything right now. Besides, I still don't totally understand that whole thing myself.

"Thanks for the ride."

He smiled brightly. "Thank you—especially for telling me about the dating thing. It's something to think about."

Now I'm back in my dorm room, and Liz isn't here. For some reason I get the impression she's been gone for a while. Hopefully to her parents'. For now I'll just enjoy the quiet and solitude as I start boning up for the end of the term and finals (just two weeks out now!).

Tuesday, November 26

Okay, I'm worried. I haven't seen Liz since last Wednesday. At first when she wasn't here on Sunday night, I thought maybe she just decided to spend an extra day at home. But when she hadn't shown up last night, I started to wonder. Now it's after eight tonight and she's still not here. I know how she says we're not supposed to "take care" of each other and everything, but I can't help but feel slightly concerned. What if something happened to her? Right now I'm torn—do I dare snoop around in her things, see if I can find any phone numbers (like her parents' home), or do I just chill and mind my own business. GOD, PLEASE SHOW ME WHAT TO DO.

Later, same night:

Well, I decided it couldn't hurt to call Rachel. I know she and Liz aren't talking these days, but she might have some idea about what's going on. Or maybe she'd tell me not to worry, that Liz is a big girl, and I'd just go back to my homework and try to forget about it.

"I haven't seen her either," said Rachel. "Of course, that's no surprise."

"Do you think I should be concerned?"

"Well, it probably wouldn't hurt to give her parents a call. And they're really nice people. I'm sure they won't mind a phone call."

"But what if Liz is there? She'll probably be furious with me for checking on her."

Rachel laughed. "Well, that's her problem, isn't it?"

"I suppose."

So I took down the number from Rachel, then went ahead and phoned Liz's parents. But here's what's got me really worried now. Liz never even went home for Thanksgiving.

"We were terribly disappointed," said Mrs. Banks. "But she said she had other plans with her friends."

Friends? Who could that possibly be? As far as I knew, Liz didn't have any friends. I cleared my throat. "Well, she hasn't come back to school yet—at least not to our room. And I was a little concerned, especially since this is getting close to finals week and all."

"Oh, dear. Do you think there's been a problem?"

"I...uh...I don't know."

"Well, has Elizabeth ever disappeared like this before?"

Now I didn't know exactly what to say. I mean, Liz

had sometimes spent the night with Jordan, but that surely couldn't be the case now. "Uh, I don't really know Liz that well," I told Mrs. Banks.

"But aren't you her roommate?"

"Well, yes. But we're...uh...not very close."

"Oh, I see." Her voice sounded more formal, as if maybe I'd offended her.

"It's not that I don't like Liz," I tried. "It's just we don't have much in common. I'm pretty involved with church and—"

"Are you a Christian?"

"Yes."

"Oh, thank God! I'd been praying that God would send someone to help my poor Elizabeth."

I felt like groaning but controlled myself. "Well, maybe that's what God did. But frankly I'm worried about your daughter, Mrs. Banks—"

"Call me Susan."

"Okay. But, really, I'm concerned for Liz. I think she's been pretty down during the last few weeks. She broke up with her boyfriend—"

"Jordan?"

"Yes. And she and Rachel aren't getting along and..." I couldn't think of anything else to say that wouldn't be too upsetting for her mom to hear.

"Well, dear, I really appreciate that you called me." I could hear a tremor of fear, or perhaps it was tears, in her voice now. "But I don't really see that there's anything you can do about this right now. Elizabeth's father and I will begin calling around immediately. We'll see what needs to be done to find her."

"Thank you. I'm so sorry to have to tell—"

"No, please don't apologize. I appreciate your concern. If Elizabeth's having any kind of trouble, I want to know about it."

"I'll be praying for her."

"You don't know how much that means to me—" she choked slightly— "to...to know that Elizabeth's been sharing her room with a...a nice Christian girl."

"I hope she's okay."

"Yes, we'll let you know as soon as we hear anything."

"Same here."

And so here I sit, wondering where in the world Liz is right now. Is she okay? I already called Kim and Lindsey to ask them to pray for her and be on the lookout, as well as to let other students know—in case anyone has seen her anywhere on campus. I also put the word out (through e-mail) for everyone I know to be praying for her. First of all, for her physical safety, and second for her spiritual well-being. I know that I, for one, will be praying myself to sleep tonight.

I can barely stand to think how totally horrible I'll feel if anything has happened to her. I mean, I know it's not my fault, but already I'm loaded with feelings of guilt. Like what if I'd only been kinder to her? Or what if I'd done this or that? Or really encouraged her to come home with me for Thanksgiving? Poor Liz. I feel like such a failure as a roommate—not to mention as a Christian.

OH, GOD, I FEEL SO GUILTY FOR NOT DOING
ENOUGH FOR LIZ. I KNOW IT WASN'T MY JOB TO
SAVE HER, BUT I COULD'VE LOVED HER BETTER. I
COULD'VE BEEN MORE PATIENT, MORE FORGIVING. I
COULD'VE GONE OUT OF MY WAY MORE. OH, GOD,
I'M SO SORRY. PLEASE, PLEASE, HELP HER. WHER-
EVER SHE IS, WHATEVER SHE'S DOING, PLEASE,
HELP HER. AMEN.

tWELVE

Wednesday, November 27 (unsettling)

Still no sign of Liz. And despite Kim's
little lecture to me today (about how it's not really my
fault), I still feel partially responsible. Not only that, but
it's been nearly impossible to concentrate on my studies.
Liz's parents are here now; they arrived this afternoon
and are staying in a hotel downtown. Mrs. Banks (Susan)
stopped by my room earlier this evening, and I told her
everything I knew that might be of help (which was very
little). They've already filed a missing person report on
her, and it's possible that the police will have to search
our room.

"I just talked to Rachel and Jordan," said Susan.
"And they really didn't know anything. It seems Elizabeth
has very few friends. Frank's driving around campus
right now. I don't know what good it'll do, but it makes my
husband feel better—like he's doing something."

"I feel so awful about this."

"The police keep assuring us that it's probably nothing, that college kids often take off without telling anyone—"

"And Liz is really independent," I assured her. "It wouldn't be like her to leave a note if she'd gone somewhere." Still, I felt worried.

Susan had tears in her eyes. "I don't know where we went wrong with her. She's probably already told you she grew up in a Christian home. But for some reason she just threw it all aside in high school. It's as if she became a totally different person—almost overnight. Her father and I have been so worried for her. But then she seemed to straighten out a little, and we were so pleased when she decided to go to college. She's very intelligent, you know."

"I know. She hasn't told me much about her past, but I sensed there had been problems." Suddenly I felt bad, like perhaps Susan thought I was suggesting that Liz's problems were family-related. "But you seem like such a nice person," I said quickly. "I can't imagine her problems were at home."

"Oh, I don't know. She became very hostile toward us during high school. We didn't have a happy home life those last couple years. Elizabeth is the youngest of our three children. Her brothers have turned out just fine." Susan twisted the strap of her purse. "I don't know what happened to make her this way. I keep praying that she'll return to God."

"So she was actually a Christian?"

"Oh, yes, she was a strong Christian, a leader among her youth group even. We never had a bit of trouble with her until high school. We thought maybe it was the school's influence, so we had her moved to a private Christian school, but things only got worse there. Within a month she was kicked out and had to return to her old school. That's about the time she and Rachel became friends. For a while I assumed that it was Rachel who was leading her astray. I don't know for sure anymore."

I was so stunned to think that Liz had been not only a Christian, but a strong Christian, that I found myself literally speechless.

"Oh, dear," said Susan. "I don't mean to make it sound like she was such a bad girl. I think she was just lost. She really has a very sweet spirit and a tender heart too."

I tried not to register the surprise I felt at this statement. After all, who knows what may have happened to Liz? How could I question her mother's image of her daughter right now when we're all feeling so worried and desperate? Besides, maybe that was the part of Liz that she kept hidden beneath her hardened exterior. "I've told everyone I know on campus that she's missing. Just in case anyone knows anything," I said weakly.

"Tomorrow we'll check with her teachers and classes to see if they might have any clues or be aware of any relationships that Elizabeth had that could be of help. I should probably call Frank to take me back to the hotel now." She looked longingly at Liz's side of the room. "The police said not to touch or disturb any of her things. But do you happen to notice anything out of place or irregular? Does it look as if she took anything with her?"

"Well, I don't see her favorite leather jacket." I glanced around. "And I don't see her backpack anywhere, so I suppose she's got those with her."

"Does she usually take her backpack everywhere?" Susan looked hopeful. "Or do you think she might have packed some things in it, perhaps like an overnight bag?"

"Well, I think she usually takes it to class. But it's possible she could've used it as an overnight bag too. I know I do that sometimes. It's not such an unusual thing to do."

Susan looked hopeful "So it's possible she's just taken off with some friends then..."

I pressed my lips together and nodded. "Sure." But I think we were both thinking this sounded slightly doubtful. Still, we needed something to cling to.

After Susan left, I got down on my knees and really prayed once again that God would protect Liz and bring her safely back. Then I tried to study, but it's no use. I'm so distracted by what may or may not have happened to Liz that I'm starting to feel slightly freaked out. Add to that the idea of the police coming here to search our room! To search for what? Do they suspect foul play or think perhaps Liz was kidnapped? And if she was, did the perpetrator break into this room? It doesn't look like anything out of the ordinary happened in here, but then you never know. And suddenly I can't stand to be in this room by myself for another minute. I'm going to call Kim and Lindsey right now and see if I can sleep on their floor tonight. Oh, my!

Friday, November 29 (give me a break!)

Well, I know I should be relieved, and I am—I really am— but at the same time I feel slightly furious. Liz is back. Since I'd planned to stay with Kim and Lindsey a few more days, until we figured out what had happened to Liz, I stopped by our room to pick up a few more things. And there she was sitting on her bed like it was the most normal thing in the world.

"Liz!" I shouted after recovering from the shock of opening the door to find someone in my room.

She looked up. "Yeah?"

"You're back; you're here. What happened to you? I mean, are you okay?"

"Well, other than getting pulled out of my psych class this morning—by the campus police, which was slightly embarrassing—I'm perfectly fine." She scowled at me. "What do you think you're doing, Caitlin? Calling in my parents and the police and God knows who—"

"I didn't call the police."

She rolled her eyes. "Well, you called my parents, didn't you?" Her voice was getting louder now.

"Yes, but I was worried. No one knew where you were and I—"

"I told you from the very beginning that I didn't want

you checking up on me! I don't need a baby-sitter!"

"I'm sorry. But what if something had happened—"

"What if? There wouldn't be much you could do about it now, would there?"

"But your parents—"

"My parents got totally freaked by your snoopy little interference. Thanks a lot!"

"Well, I'm sorry you're upset, but you might stop to think how this could upset others too. I've been barely able to concentrate on my classes this week, imagining you dead and buried out in the woods somewhere. I've been sleeping on my friends' floor and—"

"Hey, it's not my fault you got all freaked over nothing."

Right then I honestly didn't care if she totally disappeared from my life and I never saw her again. To think she could put us through all this torment, and then not even care that we were worried— I turned around and slammed my books onto my desk, grabbed a couple of things, and stormed out. I'm in the coffee shop now, but I plan to go ahead and spend the night with Kim and Lindsey again. I just needed to cool off a little first. I am so angry with Liz right now that I don't feel like a very good Christian. And I sure don't want to be around anyone until I get my feelings under control.

I ran into Liz's parents as I exited the dorm. I tried to conceal my rage from them, but I have a feeling they saw right through me. Susan introduced me to Frank. Like her, he seemed like a nice guy, mild mannered and sweet. And I could tell he'd been worried about his daughter, although I think he seemed slightly irritated too. "I'm so glad she's okay," he said. "But I wish she was better about communicating with people."

I shrugged. "She likes being independent."

"Well, anyway, we're so relieved," said Susan, grabbing my hand in hers. "And I want to thank you for your help, dear. I know how worried you must've been. I so appreciate your prayers and everything."

"Yeah." I shoved my hands into my pockets.

"We're taking Elizabeth to dinner," said Frank. "Would you like to join us, Caitlin?"

"No, thank you." I made sure I didn't say that as emphatically as I felt. NO, THANK YOU! "I've already got other plans." Yeah, plans to go fume and release some steam until I'm ready for some actual social interaction.

"Well, thank you again," said Susan, her eyes still laced with worry. "And feel free to contact us again—anytime you feel any need for concern. We know that she's an independent girl, but we still want to know what's going on."

"That's right," agreed Frank. "Anytime you notice anything out of the ordinary, you just give us a call."

"Yes, and call collect," added Susan.

"Sure," I lied. And I felt bad for lying, but at the same time I knew I wouldn't be so quick to call them again, certainly not after Liz's hostile reaction tonight. No, right now, I feel like the sooner I can get away from that girl, the better off I'll be. To think I wasted an important week—just before finals—worrying about that selfish, spiteful, malicious, mean-spirited girl! And, Liz, if you somehow got your hands on my diary and are reading it again—well, you can just be sure that I mean every word of it! And then some. Sheesh, sometimes I wish I could cuss!

Okay, I know I sound totally horrible, but it's how I feel. It's like I went way out of my way for her—I worried, I cared, I prayed—and then Liz just stomped on me! Or spit on my face! Or slapped me! I mean, how am I supposed to feel?

And suddenly I'm reminded of how Jesus may have felt when He was betrayed and beaten and finally killed on the cross. And now I feel pretty sheepish, fairly humbled, and, well, slightly foolish.

DEAR GOD, OKAY, I GIVE ALL THIS UP TO YOU—MY ANGER, MY INDIGNATION, MY FURY. YOU'VE BEEN THROUGH SO MUCH MORE. I'M SORRY THAT I'M SUCH A BIG BABY SOMETIMES. I CAN SEE THERE'S SOMETHING FOR ME TO LEARN HERE. AND WHILE I'LL ADMIT I DON'T FEEL ALL THAT EAGER TO LEARN IT, I KNOW THAT YOU KNOW WHAT'S BEST. HELP ME TO FORGIVE LIZ—AGAIN—IN THE SAME WAY YOU FORGAVE US WHEN YOU WERE TREATED SO WRONGLY. OH, LORD, I HAVE A LOT TO LEARN. THANKS FOR YOUR PATIENCE WITH ME. PLEASE HELP ME TO BE PATIENT WITH MYSELF, AS WELL AS THOSE AROUND ME. AMEN.

Saturday, November 30 (peace in the midst of yuck)

I slipped back into my room this morning, relieved to see Liz was already gone. To be honest I don't have the slightest concern about where she is or when she's coming back. Not that I'm feeling all angry right now, because really I'm not. It's just that it doesn't concern me anymore. I'm sure Liz can and will take care of herself. This is not to say that I'm not the least bit curious about where she'd been last week. Actually, I'd like to know. But do you think I'm going to ask her? Ha, think again!

Anyway I've been studying hard <u>all</u> day—making up for lost time. And I almost feel like everything's going to be okay with my finals. It's as if God has somehow reassured me, in my spirit, that He's going to help me through this—that I did nothing wrong in being concerned for Liz's welfare. And despite what she said, I believe it was right to contact her parents. So I guess I feel at peace. And that's a good feeling.

Just the same, I'm not looking forward to Liz coming home. And this makes me feel like I'm going to have to switch roommates after all. Everyone has been telling me to do it. Especially since this latest fiasco. I've decided to put myself on the list first thing on Monday. And it's fairly certain (Kim said) that I'll have a new roommate in January. Does this mean I am abandoning Liz? Not at all. As a result of all that I've been through with her (I mean, I feel I've invested myself heavily into

her life and spiritual future), I plan to keep praying for
her. And who knows, maybe once we've not roommates
anymore, she might actually want to talk to me or even
become friends. Hey, miracles can happen.

Anyway, just knowing that things will be changing
after the New Year really gives me fresh hope. And
already I'm praying that God will give me a good roommate who I can hopefully become friends with. Kim said
she'd consider switching with Lindsey, except she knows it
would really hurt Lindsey's feelings. I can see that
Lindsey already suffers from some self-esteem issues,
and I certainly don't want to contribute to them any
more. But Kim suggested that I might talk to their neigh-
bor, Jessica Knight, because it looks like she'll be losing
her roommate. Jessica's not a Christian, but she's a nice
girl who takes school seriously. She sounds like a piece of
cake compared to Liz.

But it's funny, you know, now that I feel like I'm
halfway out of here (with Liz, I mean), I'm feeling a little
sad too. Despite everything, I do feel sorry for her. And
just hearing that she'd actually been a Christian up
until high school really intrigues me. What could have possibly gone wrong? I mean, it was about the age that Liz
turned her back on God that I was just discovering Him.
And I don't know where my life would've gone if I hadn't.
It seems so ironic that she could walk away. And look
where it's gotten her. She's the most miserable person I
know. But hey, wait a minute!

Whoa! It's like the lights just came on. Of course! Now I

understand. The reason Liz is so totally miserable is because she actually knows the difference! If her mom's right and Liz really knew and loved God then turned her back on Him and walked away, she knows exactly what she's missing. Of course, that would make her totally miserable! I mean, how would I feel if I suddenly decided to chuck my relationship with God? I can't even imagine it. I'd honestly rather be dead.

Oh, man, I feel like I've just had the greatest revelation into Liz's pitiful life. From here until the end of the term, I'll really be praying for her in a whole new way. And who knows, maybe I'll even get a chance to talk to her.

DEAR GOD, WOW! I THINK YOU'VE JUST SHOWN ME THE MISSING LINK—THE KEY TO WHY LIZ IS THE WAY SHE IS. NOW I'M NOT SURE WHAT TO DO WITH IT, BUT I PRAY YOU'LL SHOW ME. SOMEHOW, PLEASE, USE ME TO UNLOCK THIS THING THAT'S MADE HER CHOOSE THE LIFE SHE'S LIVING. ALTHOUGH SHE'S NOT REALLY LIVING, IS SHE? NO WONDER SHE SEEMS LIKE THE WALKING DEAD. POOR LIZ. I FEEL MORE SORRY FOR HER NOW THAN EVER BEFORE.

OH, LORD, PLEASE PROTECT ME FROM EVER GETTING TO THAT HORRIBLE DARK AND HOPE-LESS PLACE. I KNOW I WOULD DIE WITHOUT YOU. NOT JUST SPIRITUALLY, BUT IN EVERY WAY. YOU ARE THE BREATH OF LIFE THAT SUSTAINS ME, GOD. I LOVE YOU WITH MY WHOLE HEART. AMEN.

THIRTEEN

Sunday, December 1

I went to talk to Jessica Knight this afternoon. She seemed pleased with the prospect of having me as her roommate.

"I'm not into religion or anything like that. But just the same, I don't want a roommate who smokes or drinks or parties or invites boys up." She peered at me curiously. "You don't have a boyfriend you like to...uh...entertain, do you?"

I smiled. "No, you don't have to worry about that."

"And you're not into any of that other stuff, right?"

"Not in the least."

"So then are you really into church and stuff like Kim and Lindsey next door are?" She frowned slightly.

"I'm a Christian, if that's what you mean."

"Are you one of those Christians who's bent on converting everyone within arm's length of them?"

I laughed. "Mostly I just try to live my life and be honest about it. I don't take personal responsibility for trying to save everyone I know. I figure it's up to God to do that. And if someone wants to talk about my faith, I'm always willing. But I try not to push my beliefs on unwilling ears, if you know what I mean."

"Okay, I suppose I can live with that."

"And it sounds as if we're in agreement regarding things like drinking and boys and whatever." I glanced over her shoulder to see a room that looked as if the maid had just been in. "I know that would be a huge relief to me."

"There's enough adjusting with a roommate without having a bunch of other crud tossed in. My current roommate, Cara, was a friend from high school, but there have been times when we've wanted to kill each other. I can't imagine what it would be like if you got thrown in with someone totally unacceptable." She raised her brows. "Isn't that what happened to you?"

"Well, Liz and I aren't exactly what you'd call a perfect match."

She laughed. "From what I hear, Liz would drive anyone over the edge. I heard about the catfight she and that other chick got into. Sounded pretty gruesome to me. It must be awful rooming with her."

"At least she's pretty independent. We try to stay out of each other's way most of the time."

"And didn't she go missing last week? Good grief, everyone was acting like she'd been abducted. But then it turns out she was just shacking up with her latest boyfriend. Brother!"

I felt pretty stupid just then because I hadn't heard anything about Liz having or being with a new boyfriend. "How did you hear that?"

"Cara told me. She heard it from someone."

"It would've made things a lot easier if she had just left a note or something. I know that roommates shouldn't have to baby-sit each other, but I think it's kind of nice to let each other know what's up. Like if you decided to take off for a few days, I'd hope you'd let me know."

"Yeah, same here." She smiled and stuck out her hand. "All right, Caitlin. I think this might just work out. I'll put your name down as my next roommate."

"Thanks." I smiled and told myself I should be really relieved as I went back downstairs, but I've got this tiny little nudge of a feeling—like maybe this isn't exactly the right thing after all. Although it makes absolutely no sense that I should have second thoughts about it. Everyone I know keeps telling me to lose Liz. And Jessica seems really nice. Okay, she seems _fairly_ nice. I didn't totally appreciate the way it sounded like she enjoyed dissing Liz. And yet I know that the way Liz lives is an open invitation for people to talk about her. Oh, I don't know. I guess I'll just have to pray about it.

DEAR GOD, PLEASE SHOW ME WHAT THE RIGHT THING TO DO IS. WHO DO YOU WANT ME TO ROOM WITH NEXT TERM: LIZ OR JESSICA? CAN YOU

SOMEHOW SHOW ME WHICH ONE IS BEST? I HON-
ESTLY DON'T KNOW. WHILE LIZ DRIVES ME NUTS, I
HATE TO BAIL ON HER IF YOU'VE GOT A PLAN TO
USE ME. AND I HAVE TO ADMIT THAT JESSICA IS
THE KIND OF GIRL WHO I THINK COULD GET ON MY
NERVES—MAYBE EVEN MORE THAN LIZ. YIKES! I
REALLY NEED YOUR DIRECTION ON THIS. PLEASE
GIVE ME DISCERNMENT AND CLARITY AND WISDOM.
WOW, NOW THAT'S A PRETTY TALL ORDER! AMEN.

Tuesday, December 3 (dead but not over)

Although this is "dead week" (the week before finals
and everything's due, plus you have to bone up for tests),
I feel pretty alive. After not seeing Liz all weekend, I
actually had a conversation with her last night. I'd just
gotten a new "survival package" from Mom, and I offered
to share some crackers and cheese. Then I told her how
I'd probably be rooming with Jessica next term.

She laughed. "So, I actually managed to drive you
out then?"

"I just figured it's probably the best for both of us.
Don't you?"

She shrugged and took another cracker. "I suppose.
Although it means I'll have to break in another roommate." She cussed beneath her breath. "Man, I just wish
I could afford a private room." Then she grew more hopeful. "Or maybe I'll get lucky and they won't have anyone
who's looking for a roommate for winter term."

"Not much chance of that," I told her. "I heard the waiting lists, for all the other dorms, are still pretty full too."

She cussed again.

"Hey, I hear you've got a new boyfriend." Somehow I thought this subject might cheer her up.

She scowled at me. "Where'd you hear that?"

"Jessica mentioned it. I'm not totally sure where she heard it."

"It's like there's absolutely no privacy in this stupid place. And not that it's any of your business, but John was just a fling. That's all. We met at a bar on Thanksgiving. He hadn't gone home either, and we were both feeling a little down, so we decided to make each other feel better by having a party of our own."

"Oh." Suddenly I felt sorry I'd even brought this up. Still, I hated to shut her down when she seemed to be talking so openly. Much more openly than ever before.

"Problem was the party lasted a little too long. We both got sick of each other. At least I got sick of him. And I'm pretty sure he was tired of me too. He thinks I'm too serious." She laughed. "And I think he's too flaky. Besides, he's into some stuff that I don't particularly care for."

Somehow the way she said that, I knew she meant drugs. "So he's history then?"

She held up a can of soda as if making a toast. "Yep, here's to history." Then she leaned over and studied me closely. "You know, Caitlin, I could almost like you sometimes. We'd probably even be friends if I could just get you to drink a beer or two."

Well, talk about your veiled compliments. But I decided to take it as such. "Yeah, to be honest, I'm feeling a little sad about not sharing a room with you next term."

Liz blinked. "You've gotta be kidding?"

"No, I'm still feeling a little uncertain about Jessica."

"You don't mean that redheaded Jessica, do you?"

"Yeah, she has red hair. Why?"

"And she's a sophomore, right?"

I nodded.

She laughed. "Well, good luck to you. I wouldn't last a week with someone like that."

Now I laughed. "I'm sure that's exactly what you said about me in September."

She nodded. "Yep, I did. And I was almost right too." Then she glanced at the clock. "Well, I actually need to study tonight. Thanks for the eats."

Then I went back to my desk and am now wondering what exactly transpired just now? Did aliens recently kidnap Liz and perform some sort of lobotomy on her? I mean, she definitely seems different, but maybe it's because she's so relieved to learn that I'm moving out. Still, it didn't quite seem like that. Hopefully, I'll get another chance to talk to her before next week.

Friday, December 6 (interesting evening)

Well, I did something tonight I never dreamed I'd do. But it seemed right. I invited Liz out for dinner. I figured it might be my best chance to have another good conversation with her. I was actually fairly surprised that she accepted my offer because I've heard her on the phone with Rachel this week, and they're starting to patch up their friendship again. I think it's partially a result of when Liz went AWOL (Rachel was actually pretty worried) combined with the fact that Rachel and Jordan just broke up again. And it sounds like Jordan is dropping out of school after this term. Apparently he was on academic probation and then failed to revive his grades. I feel bad for him but think it's best for Rachel and Liz.

Anyway, I knew they had some sort of plans to go out partying tonight. But Liz agreed to dinner anyway. (She arranged to meet Rachel afterward.) So we went to a new Thai restaurant that Kim thinks is good. And, amazingly, we had a pretty cool time. Relatively speaking, that is, since I sort of felt like I was picking my way through a minefield. I'd decided beforehand to do nothing more than try to be friendly to her. I simply wanted her to know that I care about her—that's all. I wasn't going to try to save her or preach at her—I just wanted to get to know her better and to love her as best I could. I thought it might actually be a new concept for her.

"Your mom said you have two brothers," I said after

we'd ordered and our tea was served.

"Yeah. They're a lot older than me. And I'm pretty sure they think I'm a spoiled brat and just slightly neurotic."

I smiled. "Your parents seem nice."

"Yeah, they're pretty nice. Remember when you thought that I came from some pitiful broken home?" She laughed. "Told you, you were wrong."

"And you know what's funny? My parents almost split up a couple years ago. They were having some serious problems."

"But they stuck it out?"

"Yeah. And they're actually both really happy now."

"Even if my parents despised each other, they'd be too afraid to get a divorce."

"Afraid?"

"Yeah, at what the church would say."

"Oh." Suddenly it got a little too quiet. "So how do you feel about your finals next week?"

She shrugged. "It'll be fine."

"When are you going home?"

"I'm not sure that I am."

"You're kidding? You don't want to go home? I can't wait."

"Yeah, I'm sure your parents just welcome you with open arms. Your mom probably cooks all your favorite dishes, and they don't even make you help clean up."

"Well, you're partly right. But I'll bet your parents are

just the same. I mean, they seem like they really love you, Liz."

She rolled her eyes. "Oh, yeah, without a doubt. They love me. But it's a pretty conditional kind of love, if you ask me."

"How's that?"

"Well, it's under the condition that someday, somehow, someway I'm going to start acting just like them."

"Like how?"

"You know. Like church stuff and all that religious rot."

"Oh." Now I considered how it seemed like she was bringing all this stuff up, not me, and so I decided to see how far she wanted to take it. "Your mom told me that you used to be pretty involved in church."

She laughed sarcastically. "Now I'll bet that really threw you for a loop. Liz Banks a church girl? Pretty weird, huh?"

I didn't admit that Rachel had hinted about the same thing. "Yeah, it was a little hard to believe. But your mom said you chucked it all during high school."

"Yep." Her face grew dark. "I realized it was all just a bunch of stupid nonsense in the middle of my junior year. And that was the end of that."

"You know what's ironic about that?"

"Oh, no." She groaned. "Here comes that sermon I knew I'd get before my time with you was over. I suppose it's the cost of the meal for me."

I laughed and held up my hands. "No, no. I'm not going to preach, I promise."

Then our meal was served. And for Liz's sake I said a silent blessing in my heart, and without missing a beat I continued. "No, I was just going to tell you about how my life was really turning into a mess during my junior year. I mean, I was partying and drinking and lying and fighting with my parents—kind of out of control."

"Hey, we could've been friends."

"Maybe. But the whole time I was unhappy."

"Okay, now here it comes. This is where you say, 'but then I got saved and my life has been just beautiful ever since.'"

"Not exactly. But you're right. I did come to know God, and He helped me make some changes in my life that have really made me a lot happier. But even so, my life's still got plenty of problems." I didn't mention how she'd been one of the biggest ones of late.

"Well, you know what, Caitlin? That's just great for you. But it doesn't work for me anymore." She took a bite of noodles then continued. "Just the same, I'm starting to realize that I've been particularly antagonistic lately, maybe even bitter, especially toward you. And I guess I'm seeing that it's not very fair. I know it's inappropriate to take out my troubles on you. I can see that now. And for that I'm sorry."

I stared at her in surprise. "That's okay."

"No, it's not okay. I mean, my problems really had nothing to do with you. And I'm sure it's just been my warped way to work out my unresolved issues regarding—you know, church stuff."

"So, have you resolved them?"

I could tell by her expression that she hadn't. "You know, Caitlin, I wanted to tell you that I'm sorry, but I'd rather not talk about this."

"Sure, no problem. No sense in spoiling a perfectly good meal. How's your Phad Thai?"

"Really good. You want to try a bite?"

And so for the rest of our meal, we managed to make fairly pleasant small talk. And if people casually observed us, I'm sure they might've assumed we were friends. Perhaps we made a small step in the direction of friendship tonight. If so, it was truly a God thing. I know I never could have orchestrated it. Still, even as I write this, I'm wondering what was it that happened to Liz to make her so bitter against the church? It seems more than just a flippant adolescent decision on her part. In fact, I'm certain something must've happened that hurt her deeply—like what I've heard Tony describe as a "mortal wound"—something that only God can heal. Was it an unanswered prayer, a deep disappointment, or perhaps something much worse? I'll probably never know since she seems pretty determined not to talk about it. Still, I feel hopeful. And I'll keep praying for her.

DEAR GOD, IT FEELS LIKE TONIGHT WAS A REAL BREAKTHROUGH FOR LIZ AND ME. AND IT MAKES ME THINK YOU MIGHT BE TRYING TO DO SOMETHING IN HER LIFE. I CAN'T IMAGINE WHAT IT IS THAT HAS WOUNDED HER SO DEEPLY, BUT I PRAY YOU'LL HELP HER TO COME TO YOU FOR HEALING. AND I PRAY YOU'LL STRENGTHEN MY RELATIONSHIP WITH HER SO THAT SHE MIGHT ACTUALLY CONSIDER ME A FRIEND.

I ALSO PRAY THAT YOU'LL MAKE IT CLEAR WHETHER OR NOT I SHOULD SWITCH ROOMMATES. AFTER TONIGHT I FEEL MORE UNCERTAIN THAN EVER. I MEAN, IF LIZ AND I COULD TALK LIKE THAT ALL THE TIME, I'D SEE NO REASON TO SWITCH. STILL, I COULD BE WRONG. PLEASE, SHOW ME WHAT'S RIGHT AND WHAT'S BEST. THANK YOU FOR TONIGHT, AND PLEASE WATCH OVER AND PROTECT LIZ AS SHE PARTIES WITH HER "FRIENDS." AMEN.

FOURTEEN

Thursday, December 12

Ahhh, my first term in college is officially over. Had my last final this afternoon. And I'm feeling pretty good about my classes too. Of course, I won't know for sure until I see my grades. Still, I'm hopeful.

Between finals yesterday, I walked past a gift shop on campus and was suddenly hit with the idea of getting Liz a Christmas present. I know it seems kind of crazy, especially when I haven't even gotten my family anything yet, plus as usual I'm penny-pinching. But then I thought, maybe God is leading me. As it turned out, I think He was. So I walked into this store with absolutely no idea what I could get her. She's the most cynical girl I've ever known, and I felt sure she'd think I was being silly or sentimental or manipulative or who knows what else to give her a Christmas present in the first place. I mean, it's just the way she thinks.

So I kept walking around, praying that God would guide me, and then suddenly I saw it. I have to admit that it seemed pretty childish, but it's like I just <u>knew</u> it was the right thing. I'd spotted this stuffed charcoal-colored lamb with a little bell on it. I picked it up and it was really soft and sweet. Still, I wasn't really convinced, especially since it looked pretty much like a child's toy, and I felt certain Liz would think this was totally juvenile. So I set the lamb down and walked away. I kept looking and looking around the store, just wasting time really because all I could think about was that goofy little lamb. Finally, I went back, picked it up, and bought it.

"Do you want it gift-wrapped?" asked the clerk.

"Sure."

"Is it for a baby?"

"No." I felt my cheeks grow warm. "Actually, it's a Christmas present for my roommate."

The woman nodded. "Oh, that's nice, dear. I'll be right back."

I felt ridiculous. Why was I buying a child's toy for someone like Liz?

So anyway, I decided I wouldn't give it to her until I leave for Christmas break. Bryce has offered me a ride home tomorrow afternoon, after he finishes his last final. I thought I'd just leave the package on her desk and quietly slip away. That way if she hated it or made fun of it, I wouldn't have to be around to feel humiliated or get mad at her.

I spent most of this evening packing up my things to

move up to Jessica's room. I thought it would be easier to do this now rather than having to scramble when I come back after the New Year. I was just taking down my photos of the Mexican kids from my bulletin board when Liz walked in.

"Hey," I called over my shoulder.

"What're you doing?"

"Just packing up to move."

She walked over and stood behind me. "I've always kind of wondered who all those kids in the photos are?"

I turned, still holding a picture of little Rosa. "These are some of the kids I tried to help when I went down to Mexico last summer and the summer before. Do you know that there are children down there who live at dump sites and actually find their food and clothes amidst the trash?" I shook my head. "And we're talking about some pretty bad trash."

"But what can you do to help them?"

"It actually doesn't take much. Showing up at the dump with something as simple as a jar of peanut butter and a loaf of bread is like Christmas for them. But some friends and I have worked to raise money to see that these kids get food on a more regular basis, and we've collected and sent clothing. Believe me, they're thankful for anything."

"Cool." She studied the photos. "I didn't realize you were such a philanthropist."

I smiled. Compliments of any kind are always so unexpected from her. And although we'd been getting along

better since our dinner date last week, I still felt a
chilly barrier between us. Almost as if she regretted
opening up to me as much as she had.

"So you're really doing it then?" she asked. "Moving
out, I mean."

"I guess so." I still wasn't entirely sure it was the right
choice, but Kim and Lindsey had both been pushing me.
In fact, they'd even offered to come down tonight and
help me cart everything upstairs.

She nodded. "Well, I figured you would. Can't say
that I blame you. I know I've been detestable at
times."

I stared at her face as she looked down at the
floor. She looked so sad and lost and vulnerable—almost
like a little girl. I didn't know what to say. "So are you
going home for Christmas then?" I asked dumbly.

She pressed her lips together then let out a long sigh.
"I don't know."

"Oh." I noticed the package I'd gotten for her, still in
its bag, next to my bed. Oh, why not? "I...uh...I have something for you."

She looked up. "Huh?"

I pulled the package out of the bag and shoved it
toward her. "Here." I forced a stiff smile to my face.

"What's this?"

"It's kind of dumb, but I just—"

"Did you know—?" She stopped herself.

"Know?"

"Oh, nothing." She was staring at the box with a

serious expression; then to my surprise she broke into a smile. "It's my birthday tomorrow."

"You're kidding!"

"Yeah. And I thought—"

"Well, happy birthday then! Aren't you going to open it?"

"You want me to?"

"Sure." I could feel my face growing warm when I imagined what she might say about the silly, childish toy. "It's really nothing, I don't even know why..."

But she was already tearing into it. And then she had the lamb in her hands and was staring at it without speaking or anything.

"Like I said, it's pretty silly. I don't know exactly why I—"

"Did my mom tell you something?" Her eyes were narrowed now, in that old familiar, hostile way, almost like she wanted to smack me or something.

"No." I took a step back. "What do you mean?"

She shook her head, her features softening some. "Oh, nothing. It's just kind of weird."

"I'm sorry. I told you it was just a really dumb impulse. You can give it away if you want—" But I stopped when I saw what looked like tears filling her eyes. Then I watched as she walked over to her bed and sat down.

I walked over and sat on my bed across from her. "What's wrong, Liz?"

She shook her head again. "It's just that this reminds me of a toy I had when I was a little girl. But I threw it away, back when..."

Somehow I knew. "When you turned your back on God."

She looked up. "How did you know?"

"Good guess, I suppose. Do you want to talk about it?"

"I don't know. I've never really talked to anyone..."

Now I got up and sat down right next to her. I'm not even sure what made me do it—I can only say that it must've been God directing me because I know I never would've done that on my own. "Liz, I know you don't really think of me as your friend exactly, but if you want to talk, I promise you can trust me."

She exhaled loudly. "Yeah. I believe I can."

"And I promise all I'll do is listen, okay? I won't try to tell you what to do or preach at you or anything. And if you want, I'll never even bring it up again."

She nodded. "It's a humiliating story—something I just wish I could forget. But I can't. No matter how hard I try I cannot wipe it from my memory." She ran her hand over the lamb's fleece. "I was really involved in the youth group at my church during my first two years of high school. I thought I was a pretty good Christian too." She looked at me. "Like you. But now I even question that. Our youth leader was this really great-looking guy in his midtwenties. His name was Glen, and I guess I was slightly infatuated with him from the start. Of course, he was married, and they had a little girl and another child on the way. But I had what I'd best describe as a schoolgirl crush. The weird thing was that Glen always seemed really interested in me too. Whenever he needed help with a project or setting up refreshments or even baby-sitting, he'd call me. And, of course, I always came running. Sometimes we'd stay after youth group just to talk and stuff. And well..." She held the lamb up to her face and closed her eyes tightly.

I could feel my heart pounding with the realization, or maybe it was just the suspicion, that something was really wrong with this story. Still, I wasn't quite sure what to say or how to say it. Finally I found my voice. "Did he touch you, Liz?"

Her eyes flashed with anger. "It was mutual, Caitlin. We _both_ 'touched,' as you put it. We _both_ got involved with each other. We had an affair, a liaison—label it what you will."

Now even though I was totally stunned, I wasn't completely surprised. Somehow it all just seemed to make sense. Still, I didn't want to shut her down. "By 'an affair,' you mean you guys had sex?"

She laughed in that cynical way again. "That's usually what it means to have an affair. We had several places where we'd meet fairly regularly. At first I didn't really like it; I mean, it felt sneaky and sort of dirty and wrong. But because I loved him, I never refused, I never said no."

"How long did it last?"

"About a year. It started early in my sophomore year and then abruptly ended at the beginning of my junior year, right after his second child was born. I know I was a fool, but I believed him. He kept telling me that he didn't love his wife and that they never talked the way we did. And he said he was going to leave her after the baby came and that when I graduated from high school he would marry me."

Liz laughed again, but it had a cold empty sound. "Okay, now you can see what a total idiot Liz Banks really was. Don't you want to laugh at me, Caitlin? I mean, think of all the horrible things I've said and done to you. Don't you want to get back at me and have a good, long laugh at my expense?"

"No." I reached over and touched her arm. "I'm sorry that it happened."

"Well, you don't need to be sorry for me. It was my own fault."

"But you were so young back then. And he was your youth pastor. What he did was wrong. He could face serious charges for that."

"See! That's exactly why I never told anyone. They would say it was all his fault, that he was the adult and I was the child. And that's not how it was."

"But you were—what—fifteen? Sixteen?"

"I was mature for my age. And I knew what I was getting into. Not only that, I enjoyed it, eventually."

Still I had difficulty believing her. "I think you truly loved Glen, Liz, but I seriously doubt that you went into that relationship looking to have sex with the man. Did you?"

She looked down at the lamb without answering.

"But I'll bet that's why he got involved with you."

She remained quiet.

"I'm not saying he's a twisted evil man. In fact, I'll bet he's got some great qualities as a youth leader and a person, or you never would've been attracted to him in the first place. But surely you can see that what he did was wrong—totally wrong. What would the pastor of your church think if he knew what this guy was up to? And whether you can see it or not, he's really messed up your life." Suddenly I remembered my promise not to speak out or preach or judge. "I'm sorry, Liz. I didn't mean to start going at you."

"No, it's okay." She looked at me with tears now running down both cheeks. "I think maybe I need to hear this."

"Okay." I took a deep breath. "Then can you see how Glen abused his leadership position in the church?"

"Well, yes. But then I allowed it to happen. Maybe I even encouraged it."

"But you were so young—he was an adult. Can't you see that?"

She shrugged.

"What if you read in the newspaper about some high school teacher who was sleeping with fifteen-year-old girls? Would you think that was okay?"

"I guess not."

"What makes it any different with your situation?"

"Oh, I don't know. I just feel like I had as much to do with it as he did. I mean, he never forced himself on me."

"Yes, but whose idea was it to start with?"

She didn't answer.

"And what makes you think he's not doing it again with some other fifteen-year-old?"

Her eyes flashed. "Oh, I don't really think—"

"Come on, Liz," I urged her. "You're a pretty sophisticated young woman. You know about this sort of thing. What do you really think? That Glen did that once but would never do it again—ever?"

"I guess I never really thought about it."

"How would it make you feel if you found out he's been pulling the same stunt with other girls?"

Her facial features drooped, and she was quiet for a moment before she spoke. "It'd make me sick."

"And why's that?"

"Because...it's wrong." Her head slumped down now, and she was crying more freely.

I'd been praying silently and desperately throughout this entire conversation, but I now prayed more fervently than ever, begging God to give me just the right words to bring this whole thing back to Him. "You know, Liz, I can't begin to imagine how that relationship must've made you feel. I mean, just thinking about it makes my head spin. You must've felt so confused and hurt and betrayed. Sheesh, it just boggles my mind!"

"Yeah, at the time I didn't know if I'd even survive it. I was so brokenhearted and hurt and disappointed. Not just in Glen, but in myself, and ultimately in God for allowing the whole thing to happen—right there in the church."

"So do you really think it was God's fault?"

"It involved a man who was supposedly serving God."

"But do you really think God was controlling Glen's actions?"

"No, of course not. I don't think God controls any of us."

"Then is it fair to blame God?"

"Oh, I don't know." She exhaled with what sounded like exasperation. "I don't even know why I told you all this."

I took a breath. "I'm sorry, Liz. I suppose I'm pushing you again. I don't really mean to do it. I just feel so bad that I want to do everything I can to make it better."

"Well, you can't fix it, can you?"

I shook my head.

"Nope, no one can."

"God can."

She rolled her eyes. "Then why hasn't He?"

"Because like you said He doesn't control you, any more than He controlled Glen. He wants you to come to Him and ask for His help."

"Well, I don't think I can do that."

"Are you happy with your life, Liz?"

She stood up now. "Happy? What is happy anyway? I'm alive, aren't I? That's something. I survived this. Now let's just forget we ever talked about this stuff. I mean, I suppose it's been somewhat therapeutic—maybe—I'm not even sure about that. And I know you're just trying to help, Caitlin. But you have to accept that you can't fix me."

"I know. I know. And I can't save you either. But I <u>can</u> be your friend, if you let me, that is. I can care about you."

I noticed her chin tremble again. "Yeah. And despite how I act, I really do appreciate that."

Then I stood up and gave her a hug. "Somehow I think everything's going to turn out just great for you, Liz. But I really believe things won't get better until you let God back into your life."

She rolled her eyes at me again. "Why am I not surprised that you would say that?" But even as she said it, I didn't sense the same hostility as before.

"Can I say one more thing?"

She shrugged. "Can I stop you?"

"Well, just for the record, I believe that Glen was an unfortunate exception among pastors. And I feel certain that nothing like that will happen in my church because both the pastor and youth pastor have what they call an 'open door policy'—they don't meet behind closed doors with anyone of the opposite sex."

She seemed to consider this. "That's probably smart."

As I stepped back I realized that I also had tears running down my cheeks. "To think all this was the result of that innocent-looking little lamb."

She laughed. "Yeah, who'd have thought?"

"Well, I should probably get back to my packing. My friends are coming down pretty soon to help me start hauling stuff upstairs."

"So, I guess you really want to move then?"

I shrugged. "Like I said, I wasn't totally sure which was best. But I sort of assumed you'd be glad to get rid of me."

"What if I promised to try really hard to be nicer?"

Now I laughed. "No offense, but is that a promise you can really keep?"

"Well, I know I'd been accused of being the wicked witch of the dorm last year...but I think I really brought out all of my artillery with you, Caitlin. I mean, as soon as I realized you were a Christian, I thought, man, am I gonna just let her have it! And I did too. Even Rachel couldn't believe how horrible I was to you. But the truth is, it never made me feel a bit better. It seemed as if it only made it easier to get meaner and coldhearted with everyone else too. And eventually it started to feel like my whole life was literally caving in on me."

"So do you really think it'll be different now?"

"Oh, I don't know...it's not as if I plan on living like a Christian again. Can you accept that?"

"Well, no one can force you to live like a Christian—that's got to come from your heart. But I guess it would make me feel better if we could agree on some rules for sharing this room."

"Well, what would it take?"

So I went over the basic things that Jessica and I had discussed, and to my surprise, Liz agreed to them all.

"Are you sure?"

She nodded. "Yeah. It'll be good for me too. My

grades aren't looking too good this term. I need to get serious about school again."

I stuck out my hand. "Okay, it's a deal then."

"Deal."

Then I groaned.

"What's wrong?"

"Now I've got to go break the news to Jessica."

She laughed. "If you think that's going to be bad, just imagine what it would've been like to live with her."

I made a face. "Sorry, Liz, but I don't think anyone could ever match your act."

She gently punched me in the arm. "You know, I'm liking you more and more."

So then I went up and told Jessica about my change in plans.

"I can't believe you." Her voice got high and shrill. "We had an agreement, Caitlin, and now you've put me in a really bad position. Who am I going to get in here at the last minute like this? I could get stuck with just anyone."

"Look, I'm sorry. It's just the way things went."

"You're seriously going to keep rooming with that creepy Liz Banks?"

I nodded.

"I guess I'm lucky then, because you must be one crazy chick yourself!" Then she actually slammed the door in my face.

So I went next door and told Kim and Lindsey about my decision. And although they were somewhat incredulous, they proved much more understanding than Jessica when I explained some of the details.

"We'll sure be praying for you," said Kim as she walked me down the hall.

"And for Liz," I reminded her.

"Yeah, you can count on that."

And so that's the plan for next term. Okay, call me a perennial optimist or a silly fool, but I think it's going to be much better than fall term. And who knows what God might do with Liz. I know that hearing her story gives me tons more compassion for her. I can't imagine what I would be like if I'd gone through the same sort of thing. Then again, I like to think I never would've gotten into that place, but you never know. You just never know.

FIFTEEN

Monday, December 16 (home sweet home)

Ahh, so good to be home. It's like having a vacation except that I'm trying to not be too much of a bum since my mom's pretty worn out from all the Christmas hoopla they've been having at her school. I've even agreed to dress up like an elf and make a surprise visit to their Christmas (oops, they don't call it that) Winter Party on Friday. And I've cooked dinner twice since I've been here. But I've also enjoyed sleeping in and hanging with my old friends. Beanie's worried that she might have to transfer from the Christian college. Apparently all her scholarship and financial aid money isn't quite enough to make it through next term. While we were doing some very frugal Christmas shopping at a new thrift shop she just discovered, she told me that she's been praying for a miracle.

"Yeah, if God wants you there, He'll make it happen."

"But it could be that God wants me back here with my mom," she said kind of sadly as she checked out the workmanship of an old beaded purse. Then she brightened. "Hey, I think she might like this."

"How's Lynn doing?"

"Okay, actually. You wouldn't believe her place. Oh, it's not exactly spotless, I mean, you know how she is, but she actually did some straightening up for me and put fresh sheets on my bed—that's a first! And she even put out some funky looking Christmas decorations."

"That's so sweet."

Beanie frowned. "Yeah, I know. But even so I find myself wishing she could've done stuff like that when I was little—it would've meant so much more then. I mean, sure, it's nice and everything, but it kind of feels like too little too late. And isn't that totally selfish of me?"

"It's probably a natural way to feel."

She shrugged. "Well, I guess I just need to remember what the real meaning of Christmas is. I mean, if you think about how Jesus came into this world—being born in a stinking stable—I really can't complain about Lynn's housekeeping." She laughed.

Then she helped me find some earrings and a bracelet for only five bucks that I know Steph will absolutely die for. Beanie is so amazing when it comes to thrift store finds!

Tonight she and Jenny and I are going out to dinner (Jenny's treat!) then to the Christmas concert at our church. We invited Anna, but she has a date with Joel

Johnson. While we were making cutout cookies at my house, yesterday, Beanie told me that she thinks they're really getting serious now.

"Does that bother you anymore?"

She laughed. "No. In fact, Joel came to visit her on campus a couple weeks ago, and he and I had a nice little chat—just friends, of course."

"Good. How's he doing?"

"Sounds as if he's doing fine. He's even thinking about transferring to our college. He said he'd like to be in a more Christian environment, but I wonder if it isn't also to be closer to Anna."

"Really? Do you think that would be good?"

"I don't know. Anna's still pretty head over heels about him. Sheesh, she even talks about marriage—"

"Marriage! She's only eighteen!"

"Nineteen," Beanie corrected me. "She turned nineteen last month."

"Still, can you imagine getting married this young?"

Beanie got a kind of dreamy look in her eyes. "Maybe."

"Maybe?" I gave her a shove, like to wake her up. "Are you nuts?"

She frowned at me. "Some people get married young and make it just fine."

I rolled my eyes at her. "I sure don't know of any." Then I studied her closely. "Just who would you consider marrying anyway, Beanie Baby?" I started to laugh. "Don't tell me you're getting interested in Danny the Drummer."

She socked me in the arm. "Very funny. No, for your information, we're just friends. And that's how I plan to keep it. Although I can't say the same for Jenny."

"So are you guys still okay?"

"Sure."

"So, who were you getting all starry-eyed over now, Beanie? You can't fool me. I know there's something going on under that mop of dark curls." We'd just put the last batch of cookies into the oven and flopped down onto the bar stools to munch on some leftover cookie dough. "Come on, tell me what's up."

"If you must know, Zach Streeter and I have been e-mailing each other lately."

"I thought you'd been doing that all along, as friends, I mean."

"Well, we stayed in touch for a while, then he had that girlfriend..."

"Oh, yeah. I forgot. Did they break up?"

She nodded.

"And?"

"And we've just had a nice time getting reacquainted is all."

"And?"

"And—and—and?" She picked up the bowl and took it to the sink.

"Come on, spill the beans, Beanie."

"And we're going out on Saturday." She stuck her chin out defiantly.

"You sure that's going to be okay?"

"I <u>knew</u> you would do this, Caitlin." She spun around and glared at me in a way that only Beanie can.

"I'm sorry." I smiled sheepishly. "Really, I am. It's just that I love you guys and—"

"And you don't want anything bad to happen to me like it did last time." She rinsed out the bowl. "Don't worry, Caitlin. I've grown up a lot in the last couple years. And so has Zach. If you must know, neither one of us is looking to sleep together—" she made a face—"you got that?"

Thoroughly humbled, I nodded. "I'm sorry, Beanie. It's really none of my business."

"You're right." She softened then. "Okay, I really do think it's because you love me."

Tuesday, December 17

Dinner with the girls and the concert was great fun last night. But the highlight of the evening was when Chloe got up there with her guitar and did a solo number singing a beautiful Christmas song she had written. It was so good that a guy who works in the music department at the local college asked her if she's interested in recording it! Well, let me tell you, that girl was ecstatic!

Apparently this guy knows her dad. But he also knows everything about rights to music and is willing to help make sure that no one tries to steal her song. And when he found out that it's just one of many, he was about ready to become her manager. Chloe was absolutely glowing. Not just with pride, mind you, but also from within. It's like God's light is really shining through her. And it's an interesting look too since she still likes wearing different kind of clothes and wears her hair in interesting styles and shades of colors (lately it's been tinted with magenta). Maybe it's just the artist at work in her. Whatever it is, I have a feeling God is going to use it in a big way!

After the concert, Josh came over to say hi and we chatted for a while. I tried not to act concerned or bothered that he hasn't been too regular with his e-mails of late. And to be honest, this was for a couple of reasons: 1) I don't want him to think I expect it of him, and 2) I keep getting this strong feeling that God is wanting me to put more emotional distance between my heart and him. So I was caught slightly off guard when he asked if I would consider going to dinner with him sometime during Christmas break.

"I...uh...I don't know," I stammered, feeling pretty silly.

"Don't worry, Cate," he assured me. "It's not like a date. I just want to talk to you and thought it would be okay to share a meal together, like two friends would do."

"Yeah." I smiled. "I'm sorry. It's just that I'm so used to nixing anything that even resembles a date."

He frowned. "What about Bryce?"

"Bryce?"

"Well, I've heard you still get rides home with him and that you guys go out for coffee sometimes. Doesn't that kind of resemble a date?"

"I guess it might to a casual observer. But I've made it crystal clear to him where I stand. And I think he respects me for it."

"But he could be in love with you."

I laughed. "Yeah, I'm sure he's just totally smitten."

"But you never know."

I shook my head. "If it makes you feel any better, he's never even tried so much as to hold my hand."

Josh nodded in a knowing way. "But sometimes your heart can get involved even when your hands are in your pockets."

I felt my face flush and wondered if he suspected that I was dealing with my feelings toward him again. Suddenly I wanted to bail on the dinner and run in the opposite direction, but before I could think of a graceful way to get out of it, Chloe joined us.

"You're amazing," I said as I gave her a quick hug. "I'm so proud of you!"

"Thanks. I can't believe what a big deal everyone's making over it. It's just a little song."

"Hey, Sis," said Josh in a big-brotherly way. "Don't knock it, or it's like you're knocking God. You've obviously got a real gift, and you need to remember that He's the one who gave it to you."

I glanced uneasily at her, hoping she wouldn't take it the wrong way, but to my relief she just smiled. "You know what, Josh? You're right. I need to remember to give God the glory when someone compliments me."

Then we all started drifting off our separate ways,

and I never did get a chance to bail on dinner. Still, we never set an actual date. Maybe he'll get too busy or simply forget. Or maybe I'll come up with a good excuse.

DEAR GOD, I FEEL LIKE YOU'RE TRYING TO TELL
ME SOMETHING IN REGARDS TO JOSH, BUT I'M
JUST NOT COMPLETELY SURE WHAT IT IS. AND I'M
NOT SURE IF IT'S RIGHT OR WRONG TO GO TO
DINNER WITH HIM. MAYBE IT'S NEITHER. PLEASE
SHOW ME WHAT'S BEST TO DO. THANK YOU. AMEN.

Friday, December 20 (what's going on?)

After putting in a long afternoon as an elf (complete with green tights and pointy hat, which I still had on), I arrived home with my mom to see a nice silver BMW parked in front of our house. "Anyone you know?" I asked Mom as I helped her carry a box full of Christmas stuff into the house.

"Nope. Nice wheels though."

Well, we'd barely stepped into the house when I heard Josh's voice. "Ben let me in," he explained quickly. "We were just playing a video game, but the phone rang and he got it." He glanced at my strange outfit. "Cool threads, Cate."

"Thanks." I set down the box.

"Hey, Josh," said my mom as she hung up her coat. "Long time no see. How's it going?"

"Great." He smiled that bright smile, and I could tell

he had Mom right in the palm of his hand. "Sorry to drop in like this, but I was just passing by, and your daughter promised to go out to dinner with me sometime." He glanced at me. "And I was thinking about tonight. If you're not too busy, that is."

"Oh, she's not busy," my mom answered for me, then laughed. "Sorry, Caitlin, I didn't mean to speak for you. But you've been such a good little elf today, and you already cooked dinner two times for us this week. I think you deserve a night out, don't you?"

Well, what was I going to say? And, besides, it seemed pretty silly to pass up a perfectly good dinner with a guy who I really have enjoyed being friends with. "Sure. But do you mind if I change first?"

"Oh, do you have to?" pleaded Josh with a twinkle in his eye. "I thought maybe I could dress up like Santa and we could get a holiday discount on our meal."

I laughed. "Maybe at McDonald's. Hey, is that your car out there?"

"No way. It's my mom's latest. My Jeep's in the shop right now; she let me borrow it."

"Nice."

So I went up and changed into a burgundy sweater dress that seemed to go with his sports jacket and khakis. Then we drove to the city in his mom's really cool car to a new and rather uptown restaurant that's pretty expensive.

"Get anything you like," he said after, I'm sure, he noticed my eyebrows go flying up over the prices—and in some instances lack of prices—on the oversized menu.

"What's the big occasion?" I asked.

"Just two old friends spending some quality time together."

I nodded. "Okay. I can live with that. Jenny treated Beanie and me to dinner this week. I guess it's nice having all these rich friends."

He laughed. Then I proceeded to tell him the latest on my roommate (not all the details about the corrupt youth pastor) but mostly about the little lamb and our surprising last-minute reconciliation. I'd kept him posted off and on during the ups and downs of living with Liz, but I hadn't told him anything lately.

"I wonder if it's really wise to keep rooming with her."

"I know. I was a little worried too. But she promised me that things are going to be different now."

"I hope so. She sounded a little scary to me."

"Yeah. She was. But I really think God is up to something in her life. I think she's trying to come back to Him."

"Well, let's hope so. I'll keep praying for her."

We continued chatting casually throughout the meal, and I began to wonder what had had me so troubled before. This was, as Josh had promised, just two old friends getting together to talk.

"Josh, this was so great," I told him as the waiter cleared away our entrees. "Thanks."

"You don't want dessert then?" He looked hopeful.

"I couldn't eat another bite. But I wouldn't mind some coffee."

He ordered something I couldn't pronounce and two
coffees, and suddenly he seemed to get slightly serious.
"You know, Caitlin, I wanted to talk to you about something—" he cleared his throat—"something important
tonight."

"Sure. What is it?" Suddenly I wondered if he was
going to launch into a sermon about how it wasn't wise for
me to spend time with Bryce, but I kept my face completely blank.

He leaned forward. "I'm not quite sure how to say
this, but let me just cut to the chase. There was a cus-
tom back in the Bible days where people who were
attracted to each other entered into a kind of
covenant."

I could feel my heart rate speeding up. What in the
world was he talking about?

"I know, it probably sounds strange—especially in
these days—but stay with me for a minute, okay? You
see I wrote a term paper on it in my Old Testament class,
and it suddenly started to make sense to me."

The waiter set down our coffees, and I pretended to
focus my attention on my cup, although my hand was
starting to shake just slightly.

"Anyway, I'll try to get to the point. Caitlin..." He
paused as if waiting for me to respond.

I looked up at him. "Yes?" And then I saw it in his
hand—a small, dark blue velvet box. And I honestly
thought I was going to faint and fall out of my chair.
What _was_ he thinking?

"You and I are so much alike, Catie, and it's no secret that I've been in love you with you ever since high school."

I know my eyes must've been about as round as the coffee cup, but I was absolutely and totally speechless. It's like it was all a dream or something.

"And I want to ask you, not to exactly become engaged to me, but to make a covenant with me, that I believe will lead to engagement and then marriage." He held out the box. And not knowing any better I let him set it in my hand. What in the world do you do in this particular situation? Do you answer the guy? Do you open the box? Or what?

"Go ahead, open it," he urged. "It's a covenant ring. Like a promise to become engaged."

So I opened the box to find, not a huge sparkling solitaire, but a simple golden ring with a cross engraved on the front. "I...uh...I don't know what to say, Josh," I finally muttered.

"Do you need to think about it?"

"I'm just so stunned." I looked at him, immediately noticing the disappointment creeping into his eyes. Of course, he'd expected a different reaction than this. I studied him for a long moment. "There's no denying that I love you, Josh. I think you've always known it. But this is just so—so surprising."

Now he smiled just a little. "Yeah, I guess I've had a lot more time to think about all this than you have. But it really makes sense to me. I know we're both too young to get married right now, but at the same time, I feel totally certain that you're the one for me. And in a way that's become a big distraction to me—thinking of you and worrying that some Prince Charming will gallop into your life and sweep you off your feet."

I laughed. "Yeah, sure."

"So what do you think?"

"I don't know what to think, Josh. I'm still in a state of shock."

"It wouldn't change anything as far as the vows we've made to God. All it does is show everyone that we've been set aside for each other. Does that make sense to you?"

I nodded, a smile slowly growing on my face.

"Are you willing to make this kind of covenant with me?"

"I...uh...I think so, Josh. But I'd like to pray about it first."

"Oh, yeah. Of course." Then he slipped the ring from out of the velvet lining. "Do you want to see if it fits? I told the jeweler that I thought you had small fingers." He laughed. "So he made it in a small size, but he said it could be stretched bigger if necessary."

"Which hand do I—?"

"Maybe the left, like an engagement ring."

The ring was a little tight, but it went on. "It's nice, Josh."

"Well, go ahead and wear it then. And pray about this whole thing, and even talk to your parents about it. I almost considered asking your dad first, like in Jewish tradition, but since this was a covenant, not an official engagement, I just wasn't sure."

I could feel tears building in my eyes as I stared down at the delicate ring. Part of me was wildly happy, but another part of me was uncertain and just slightly frightened.

"Was I wrong to ask you this, Caitlin?" His eyes were wide with sincerity.

"No. I don't think so. It's just that it's taken me so much by surprise. I don't know how to act."

"Just act like yourself. And don't worry; I don't expect a thing from you. Really. I don't even want to kiss you good night."

"You don't?"

"Well, I guess I said that wrong. Of course, I'd love to kiss you. But I know that it's not the right thing to do right now."

Somehow hearing him say that was something of a relief. But still, as I sit here and write all this down, I feel confused and shocked and happy and sad and thrilled and worried and so many other emotions I can't even begin to understand it all. I haven't said a word of this to my parents yet. First, I want to really pray about the whole thing. I want to know what God thinks about this. More than anything I really want His will. And so I'm hitting my knees right now.

DEAR GOD, PLEASE SHOW ME YOUR WAY...

SIXTEEN

Monday, December 23

It's been three long days since Josh's "proposal"—I can't think of what else to call it, although proposal seems a bit overstated. The first day, I kept mostly to myself. I took a walk in the park and really prayed that God would show me His will. And I have to admit that part of me was really excited about the whole thing. I wanted to run over to Beanie and Jenny and show them my ring and hear them squeal and get excited. (At least that's how I thought they would react.) But I controlled myself and spent most of the day alone with God and my Bible. By the afternoon, I felt just as confused as I had before.

But then I read a verse in Proverbs (actually I'm sure God showed it to me because it literally popped off the page). Anyway, it's the verse about how you can find wisdom with "many advisers." So, I decided it was time to ask for advice. Since I still consider Tony to be my pastor, I called him but got Steph instead (also a good counselor). I told her I had a problem that I wanted some help with, and she invited me over for dinner that night.

Just as we were finishing dinner, I explained what had happened with Josh a couple nights ago.

"That Josh is such a considerate young man," said Steph as she wiped Oliver's face and excused him from the table. "I've never heard of a covenant exactly like that, but it sounds like a nice idea."

Tony was holding baby Clay and finishing up his last bite of lasagna. "I'm not so sure," he said as he laid down his fork.

"What do you mean?" asked Steph.

"Well, I don't really see any difference with what Josh is proposing and an official engagement."

"The way he explained it was that it's supposed to be similar to how it was done in Bible times. The man would make an agreement with the woman's family that they would marry later on—sometimes many years later like with Jacob and Rachel."

"Yeah, I can see that," said Tony. "It's just that I would call that agreement or contract or whatever the same as an engagement."

I considered that. "Well, I suppose it sort of is."

"So why not call a spade a spade?" Tony shifted the baby and leaned back into his chair. "I don't mean to pick on Josh; you know I think he's a fine young man. But I don't quite understand this."

"He's in love," said Steph, still caught in the romance. "But he knows they're too young to get married yet."

"Are you in love with him?" asked Tony, eyeing me closely.

I felt my cheeks growing warm. "Yeah, I think I have been for a long time."

"So then what's really the problem here?" I could feel Tony still studying me.

"I'm not sure. On one hand, I think it's wonderful. But on the other, I feel—I don't know—hesitant, I suppose."

"Well, it's probably because you are so young," said Steph. "You're probably just overwhelmed."

I nodded. "I think that's a big part of it. It's like too much too soon."

"Just tell Josh how you feel." Tony smiled. "He should understand."

"Then am I saying no to him?"

Steph frowned. "He might feel like you are. Do you want to say no?"

"I don't know." I put my hands on my face and groaned. "That's the problem; I just don't know."

"And you've been praying about it?"

"Yeah. But I still feel confused."

"Well, you know what they say," said Tony lightly. "When in doubt, don't."

"Oh, Tony." Steph scowled. "You make it sound so easy. What if you were in Caitlin's shoes? What if you loved someone but just weren't sure?"

He laughed. "That doesn't work for me, honey. When I

fell in love with you, I didn't have the slightest doubt that you were the one for me."

Steph smiled. "You old romantic."

"Maybe I should leave," I said, suddenly feeling like the fifth wheel.

"No, no," said Steph as she began to clear the table. "I feel as if we haven't really been much help to you."

I helped her clear and Tony followed us into the kitchen. "Caitlin," he began. "You are a wise young woman, and I know you have a heart to follow and obey God. And you're doing the right thing to ask for advice, but I have a feeling God is already leading you—in your heart. You just need to be willing to really listen and obey."

"I am."

He nodded. "I know you are."

"Does that mean I shouldn't ask for any more advice?"

"No, you're absolutely right to ask for advice. Proverbs 11:14 spells it out pretty plainly—it is good to seek out counsel from a number of people who you love and trust."

"Have you talked to your parents yet?" asked Steph.

"No, you guys are the first."

So later that night I talked to my folks. At first they were all kind of shocked and upset. "You're too young to be thinking about marriage," said my dad.

"Josh is a nice boy," said my mom. "But do you really want to tie yourself to just one guy?"

"You're only eighteen," said my dad, like I might've forgotten my age. "You both need to finish college—"

"I know," I said in a somewhat irritated voice. "We're not talking about getting married—"

"Then why this—this engagement?" asked my dad.

"It's not an engagement."

"Call it what you want, but it sounds like an engagement to me." Dad frowned. "And if Josh is so set to follow biblical examples, why hasn't he come and talked to me? I think this was something that fathers decided."

"Yeah, Josh mentioned that. And he plans to. He just wanted to see how I reacted first."

"That sounds sensible." My mom smiled. "Really, honey, it's your decision as to whether you feel it's right to become engaged or not. Whatever you decide, you know that we'll support you 100 percent."

My dad made a harrumph noise.

"Dad, you seem pretty upset by this."

"I'm sorry." He softened. "It's just that you're so young, Catie. You're my little girl."

I laughed. "I'll always be your little girl, Daddy. That's just the way it is, right?"

He nodded sadly. "Yeah, but I guess I'm just not ready to share you yet."

"Well, I'm not ready to run off and get married yet."

"Are you ready to be engaged?" he asked. "Is it what you really want?"

"I'm not sure. Most of all I want to do what God wants."

He smiled. "I'm sure you'll do the right thing. Like your

mom said, we trust you. You're a good girl, and you haven't let us down yet. Whatever you decide, I'll try to be happy for you. It might take a little time and adjusting on my part—but in time I'll be happy."

The next day I went to the Christmas Eve service at church and naturally saw Josh. "So?" he said expectantly after the service ended.

I smiled. "Can you be patient with me? I'm still thinking about the whole thing—it's really a big decision, you know. Next to becoming a Christian this will be the biggest decision of my life."

"I'm glad you're taking it seriously, Cate." He nodded. "It's one of the many things I really love about you."

Then he asked me to go to lunch with him, but I had to tell him no since I'd already made plans to spend the afternoon with Beanie and Jenny. I planned to break the news to them and see what they thought. Okay, I realized they might not be the oldest and wisest of counselors, but I believe they love me and will tell me what they really think. As it turns out, they did.

"Josh did what?" exclaimed Beanie after I briefly told them the story over tacos.

"You're kidding!" cried Jenny. "I can't believe it! You guys are going to be the first ones to actually tie the knot."

"I haven't agreed to anything yet."

"Good thing," said Beanie. "It sounds crazy."

"But you were just talking about how marriage was sometimes okay—"

"Oh, I was just talking." Beanie shook her head. "I wasn't serious. You're way too young, Caitlin. We're all too young. Good grief!"

"Well, we weren't actually planning on getting married." I sighed. "I don't know why no one seems to get this. It's just an agreement that we'll become engaged."

"Sounds more like an engagement to me," said Jenny. "And for the record, I think it's cool."

"Really?"

"Yeah, why not?"

"Would you do it?"

Jenny laughed. "With Josh you mean?"

I felt my face redden as I suddenly remembered that she and Josh were once an item, just a couple of years ago. "No, not with Josh, silly!"

"Well, if I really loved the guy and felt he was the right one. Sure, why wouldn't I?"

"I don't know. But for some reason I'm still not totally sure."

"That's because it's a _bad_ idea," said Beanie, shaking her finger at me. "A very bad idea."

"How can you be so sure?"

"I just feel it in my bones."

Now I laughed. "And what does that mean? Have you suddenly become the village wise woman, and you just feel these things in your bones?"

She smirked at me. "No, but for some reason it doesn't feel right."

"You're just jealous," chided Jenny.

"Jealous?" Beanie glared at her. "Jealous of what?"

Jenny raised her brows. "I don't know. Maybe you're feeling possessive of Caitlin—maybe you don't like the idea of her growing up and getting married. Maybe you're afraid she'll leave poor Beanie Baby behind."

Beanie punched her in the arm.

"Ouch!" complained Jenny. "Lighten up, Beanie, I'm just kidding."

"Come on, you guys. I didn't tell you this so we could all get in a big fight. I was just looking for some advice."

Jenny held her thumb up. "I say, if you really love him, then go for it."

But Beanie held her thumb down. "I say it's too soon."

And so now I'm feeling about as confused as I was to start with. Beanie's advice sounds a little flaky after she was just acting all sweet and starry-eyed about Zach and the idea of getting married young. I mean, here Josh and I aren't even talking about marriage or even an official engagement, and Beanie gives me a thumb's down. On the other hand, Tony didn't seem so enthused about the whole thing either. And my dad sure wasn't. Still, everyone (except for Beanie!) pretty much agreed that it was my decision. So I guess I'm right back where I started. It's still between me and God.

DEAR GOD, I'M BEGGING YOU, PLEASE, SHOW ME WHAT THE RIGHT THING TO DO IS. I FEEL SO CON-FUSED. AND YET I HAVE TO ADMIT THAT I LIKE THE LOOK OF THIS LITTLE GOLD BAND ON MY FIN-

GER. AND YOU KNOW THAT I LOVE JOSH. SO,
PLEASE, TELL ME, WHAT WOULD BE SO WRONG
WITH ENTERING INTO THIS COVENANT WITH HIM? I
THINK IF I WERE OLDER (SAY 21 EVEN), I'D PROBA-
BLY JUMP AT THE CHANCE AND SAY, "YES! YES!
YES!" AND SO I'M WONDERING WHAT'S WRONG
WITH US BEING COMMITTED TO EACH OTHER LIKE
THIS FOR THE NEXT THREE OR FOUR YEARS?
SHEESH, JACOB AND RACHEL WERE ENGAGED FOR
SEVEN YEARS, AND THEN I THINK THEY HAD TO
WAIT FOR ANOTHER SEVEN AFTER HER DAD
TRICKED JACOB INTO MARRYING THE OLDER SIS-
TER. GOOD THING I DON'T HAVE A SISTER. BUT
REALLY, GOD, PLEASE SHOW ME WHAT TO DO.
AMEN.

SEVENTEEN

Friday, December 27

Well, life has been a whirlwind of activity lately. What with all the preparations for Christmas and then the actual celebrations, including taking the part of an angel in the church's living nativity when Andrea LeMarsh got the flu, I've neglected my diary. But here's what happened.

After the Christmas Eve candlelight service at church, I told Josh that I wanted to enter into this covenant with him. I explained that it was a hard decision and that I still felt a little strange about it (because it feels like we're awfully young), but that if he was willing to wait three or four years (or maybe even more), then I was willing to do the same. Well, he was elated. He threw his arms around me and was almost (I think) about to kiss me, when he stopped himself.

"Now I promised you we wouldn't get physical or kiss or

anything and I intend to keep that promise, Caitlin. Are you okay with that?"

"Sure." I smiled. And so we shook hands. We told my parents that night (when he brought me home), and although they seemed a little surprised, they both handled it well. Then the next evening he took me over to his parents. But I was pretty worried on the way over there.

"Are they going to be okay with this?" I asked.

"I've been preparing them for it. But they don't quite get it. My dad thinks we're just making a big deal about going steady."

I laughed nervously.

"And my mom is concerned that we're tying ourselves down unnecessarily. I think those were her exact words."

"How about Chloe? I haven't had a chance to talk to her."

"Chloe's totally cool with it. She told me she always wished that it would happen. And she doesn't even think we're too young."

I laughed. "Well, that coming from a fifteen-year-old."

"A mature fifteen-year-old."

"Yeah, you're right."

And so we had coffee and dessert with Josh's parents. Everyone acted nice and civilized and everything, but I couldn't help but get the feeling that they thought Josh and I were just playacting at being grown-ups or something. Still, I tried not to think about it too much.

And then tonight Josh took me out to dinner again at the same restaurant. It was actually really romantic (although we're still not kissing or anything), just being together and talking about what our futures might be. I told him how I still really want to do something for the orphans in Mexico—but not only for them, but perhaps for kids all over the world. I told him about Kim and her plans to be a social worker.

"I don't know exactly what God has in store for us, Caitlin, but I can sure see why He's put us together."

I smiled. "Yeah, it feels right, doesn't it?"

And so I should be ecstatically happy right now. Shouldn't I? I mean girls are usually thrilled to get engaged—and isn't that sort of what this is? But to be perfectly honest, I still have this little nagging feeling that something's not exactly right. I've prayed and prayed and never felt God pushing me one way or the other. And I know there's nothing wrong with what Josh and I have agreed to. As long as it's right, that is.

Oh, I suppose I'm just obsessing. That's what Jenny said. She thinks what we've done is totally cool. Not so with Beanie, though. She's furious at me. She thinks I'm blowing it big-time. My one consolation is that Beanie's the only one who thinks this. And as much as I love Beanie, she can be sort of a loose cannon sometimes. I mean, she hasn't always used the greatest judgment in her own life. How can I trust what she thinks in regard to mine?

Friday, January 3 (back to school)

Well, I'm back at school now. Josh actually drove me here yesterday. It was so sweet of him since it's so far out of his way, but he insisted. He also made me promise not to get rides home with Bryce anymore.

"But I don't know anyone else who lives near us," I complained. "And that means my parents will have to come to get me—"

"Or I will."

"But it's so far."

"Not too far for you."

I smiled. "Well, if you really don't mind."

We went out with Beanie and Zach on New Year's Eve and had a really great time. It's funny because it feels like we've all really grown up since the last time we did something together. And it was so cool! It helps to know that Beanie's actually getting over her earlier frustration with me for this whole Josh thing. Although she made it perfectly clear afterward that she still doesn't think it's a very good idea.

"But I've come to the conclusion that it's your decision, not mine," she said as we downed some cocoa up in my room. "And if you think it's right, then who am I to disagree." She made a face. "Even though I do!"

I haven't told anyone at school about Josh and me yet. I sort of wanted to tell Liz first. I'm not even sure why. But she hasn't even gotten back. I'm assuming she went home, but I don't know for sure. I do know that I'm not going to call the campus police and report her as missing. Besides, it looks as if she packed up and left the room in an orderly manner. I'm actually looking forward to seeing her again. In fact, it feels rather lonely here right now. I almost wish that I hadn't let Josh bring me back on Thursday. (He had to come then in order to be back at his own school in time for registration). My parents had offered to bring me back on Sunday so that I could have a few more days at home, but I thought it was more important to spend that time with Josh. And it's too late to change things now.

Sunday, January 5

Liz came back today. She'd spent the first week of the break at her parents, but the remainder was spent at her grandparents' winter home in Palm Springs. Needless to say, she came back with a nice tan!

"You look great," I told her as soon as she walked in the door.

"I feel pretty good too." She unloaded her bags and then dug around until she found a package wrapped in brown paper. "This is for you."

"Really?" I felt the small package. "What for?"

"Late Christmas present."

"Thanks." I unwrapped the bundle to find what appeared to be a handmade silver cross pendant with a turquoise stone in the center. "This is beautiful!" I exclaimed.

She smiled. "It's made by the Pueblos. I found it at a flea market with my grandma. She said it could be pretty old. I thought you might like it."

"I love it." Immediately I put it on. "Thanks so much."

She laughed. "I thought it might help to protect you from me. You know what they say about silver crosses and all."

"So are you like saying you're a vampire?"

"No, but living with me has probably been a lot like living with the devil."

"But I thought things are supposed to be changing for us."

"I hope so. But you never know. I'm sure I could still get pretty witchy if the occasion called for it."

"Well, hopefully it won't."

Then Liz told me that she confided in her mom about what had happened to her back in high school with the youth pastor. "I hadn't really planned to tell her, it just sort of slipped out one day."

"I think that's good," I said. "It's important that someone in the church knows about it."

She shrugged. "I don't know if my mom really believed me."

"Well, maybe she was just shocked. It is pretty shocking, you know."

"I guess. But I'd always suspected that she'd known about it back then."

"I don't know. Parents can be pretty dense sometimes. Plus I think they want to think the best about their kids."

"I suppose. But it was pretty uncomfortable once I'd told her about it. That's why I decided to shoot on down to Grandma's house for the duration of winter break."

"Well, your mom probably needs time to think about it and sort it all out. Do you think she'll do anything?"

Liz groaned. "Ugh, I really don't want to think about that. I'm still not even sure why I told her. The truth is, I hope she just forgets the whole thing."

Well, I hope she doesn't! Naturally, I didn't tell Liz this. But that whole thing really, really bugs me! And it seems like someone should check into that creepy youth pastor. I'm really praying that Liz's mom will be the one to do it.

I considered telling Liz about Josh then, if only to gracefully change the subject, but somehow it just didn't feel right. It's not that I thought she would laugh at me, exactly, but she might react like Beanie. Or she might think the whole thing was silly and childish, like going steady in grade school. Anyway, for whatever reason, I haven't said anything to anyone here yet.

I did get a sweet e-mail from Josh today. It sounds like he's taking a really full load of classes during winter term. He said that was the best time to load them on since there wasn't much else to do, plus winter term is just slightly shorter than the others. Anyway, I'm thinking maybe I'll follow his lead and take more. Despite what my adviser told me last term, I went ahead and took fifteen hours (she said to take it easy my first term). But I did just fine and my grades were even better than I expected. So maybe I'll add another class next week.

Friday, January 10 (back to the grind)

Wow, I've really given myself a full load of classes. And suddenly I'm wondering if that wasn't too smart. I'm taking seventeen hours, and some of the classes sound like they could prove challenging. Still, I want to give it a shot. It's not as if I have a lot else going on in my life. And at this rate I could possibly graduate early—maybe even in three years! Now that would be something.

I went ahead and told Liz about Josh. She noticed the ring when we went out for coffee last night. Yes, we actually went out for coffee! It's the second time we've done something like that together (counting when I took her out for dinner before Christmas).

"You probably think it's crazy," I said when she didn't respond right away.

"I don't know." She shook her head. "It does seem kind of strange. I don't think I'd like it very much if a guy pulled something like that on me."

"Like what?"

"Oh, you know, some sort of binding agreement that you won't see anyone but him, and he's hundreds of miles away. I mean, what happens if you meet someone who really interests you?"

"Oh, that wouldn't—"

She laughed. "Of course, it wouldn't. You'd never

allow it to. But how can you live like that, Caitlin? Don't you feel sort of confined?"

I considered her words. Right now I don't want to do anything that comes across as judgmental or might shut her down. "I don't know. To be honest, I still feel a little weird about the whole thing."

She pointed her finger at me. "See. That's a bad sign. If it's the right thing, you should feel really good about it."

"But feelings can be misleading."

She shrugged. "Well, before anyone ever gets me to make a commitment like that, I want to feel good about it."

"Oh, I feel good—"

"But not completely, right?"

"I'm not sure."

"Yeah, this is probably the exact reason that I don't think I'll ever get married."

"Really? You don't think you'll get married someday?"

She shook her head. "Nah. Why bother?"

"But don't you want someone who loves you so much that he's willing to commit himself completely to you?" Even as I said it, I wished I hadn't. I'd almost forgotten about her affair with Glen the youth pastor. She had said that she was totally in love with him. And look what that had done to her.

"I don't mean to hurt your feelings, Cate, but I don't think that kind of love really exists. I mean this Josh fellow might act like he loves you now, but I think he's just trying to keep you under his thumb. And I personally wouldn't appreciate a guy who wanted to do that to me. Nope." She held up her cup. "I'd rather be free."

Well, I wouldn't admit it to anyone, not even Liz, but something she said made sense to me. I just can't quite put my finger on it. Still, I need to remind myself where she is coming from. Sheesh, it was only a month ago when I thought she was the closest thing to the devil himself!

Wednesday, January 15 (word's out)

I went to fellowship group tonight—their first official meeting since Christmas break. It was fun but kind of weird. Or maybe I'm the one who's weird. I walked over there with Kim and Lindsey, and I decided it was finally time to tell them about Josh. I showed them the ring, and Kim let out an appropriate squeal.

"That is so cool," she said. "I barely knew Josh last year, but he's so good-looking. And that smile. Honestly, if he wasn't bent on being a pastor, I'll bet he'd have a good chance in Hollywood."

I laughed. "Yeah, I used to imagine he looked like Matt Damon."

"Oh, he's cuter than that." Kim slapped me on the back. "Well done, Caitlin!"

"I don't know," said Lindsey.

Here we go, I thought. It seems that everyone always has a differing opinion about this. I'll bet if I took a vote it would be a clean split—fifty-fifty.

"What do you mean?" demanded Kim. "Aren't you excited for Caitlin?"

"But they seem so young." Lindsey sounded apologetic. "I mean, I realize you're just a year younger than me, but I think even I'm too young—"

"Maybe you are," interrupted Kim. "Some people mature faster. And I think Caitlin and Josh are both pretty mature."

"I suppose." Lindsey shrugged. "But I still think you should wait before making a commitment like this."

"So," began Kim in a challenging voice, "if, let's say, Stephen were to ask you to do something like—"

"Oh, stop it, Kim!" exclaimed Lindsey. "That's just stupid."

"No, it's not. You and he have been dating, and I know you really like him. What if it suddenly developed into something serious and Stephen handed you that little velvet box? Are you telling us that you'd turn him down because you're too young?"

"Oh, I don't know. This whole conversation is just totally ridiculous."

Then Kim started laughing. "You see, Caitlin, she'd be singing a different song if she were in your shoes."

"Yeah, I'd be screaming," laughed Lindsey. "Because Caitlin's shoes would be at least three sizes too small!"

Then we all laughed. But still, something about Lindsey's comments and then the way Kim announced to everyone that I was "next to engaged to Josh Miller" just sort of made me uncomfortable. Especially when Bryce came up and asked me if it was true.

"Yeah. It really took me by surprise, but then Josh and I have been close friends for the last couple of years."

"But what about that whole nondating thing?"

"Oh, we haven't been dating—not each other or anyone else, for that matter. But somehow Josh felt it was time to make a commitment like this."

Bryce looked slightly puzzled. But he told me congratulations and shook my hand. And no way did I have the heart to tell him that Josh had asked me not to catch rides home with him anymore. I'll deal with that later. Still, it sort of makes me sad.

And I have to admit that this whole thing made me feel like an outsider tonight. Or maybe it's just because I don't know everyone as well as the others. But, no, I think it's more than that. I feel like I don't belong there, somehow, like being "the closest thing to engaged" sort of sets me apart and isolates me from them. Am I imagining this, or is it really true? And if it is true, then isn't it just as Josh had planned? Like we're setting ourselves aside for each other? And shouldn't that be a good thing? But if it's a good thing, then why doesn't it feel good? Too many questions and not enough answers—it must be time to go to bed.

EIGHTEEN

Friday, January 31 (winter weary)

For some reason this has been the longest month. It doesn't help that the weather's been lousy—foggy and icy and miserable. Plus, now I'm sure I took too many classes because I'm feeling slightly stressed and overloaded. On top of that it seems as if everyone else is having a life except for me. Liz is out with her latest guy Conrad tonight. He's actually kind of nice and treats her way better than Jordan ever did. And here's what's amazing: I don't think she's even sleeping with him! Not that it's any of my business or that I want it to be, but last week Liz asked me if I'd ever slept with a guy. And I just came right out and told her why I hadn't and wouldn't until my wedding day.

"You've got to be kidding," she said. "You and Josh don't plan to at least test each other out before you tie the knot?"

"Nope."

"That's crazy! What if you can't stand each other in bed?"

I laughed nervously. "I don't think that's going to happen. I believe when God puts two people together like that, it'll all work out."

"But what if it doesn't?"

I smiled. "It will."

She shook her head. "Well, you're one brave girl."

"Why would waiting until my wedding day be any braver than doing it with a guy right now? I mean, I think people who get sexually involved without the commitment of marriage are the brave ones." I laughed. "Or the foolish ones."

She scowled at me.

"I'm sorry. But it's just how I see it. To me it seems really risky to be involved in casual sex. Honestly, I just don't get it. I'd rather wait and have it be really special with just one man—the one I love and am willing to spend my life with—and on my wedding night."

She rolled her eyes. "Yeah, the old fairy tale—and you'll live happily ever after, right?"

"Oh, I'm sure there'll be some bumps along the way. But you can't tell me that the choices you've made regarding sex have made your life all peachy and wonderful."

"Maybe not. But there's not much I can do about my mistakes now—other than to hopefully learn from them."

I smiled. "Well, learning from them sounds pretty smart."

"And I'm sure if I need any advice on how to keep myself sexually pure, you'll always be ready and willing to dish it out, right?"

I laughed. "You bet. Bring it on! And if I don't know the answer maybe I can just make something up."

She smiled. "Yeah, I'll bet you could."

Now what I'm actually hoping and praying will happen is that I can share a little bit about Beanie's story—how she gave up her virginity and subsequently got pregnant. Then she recommitted herself to God, and now believes He's restored her virginity. I know some people don't quite get this, but I'd like to see Liz's reaction. Who knows, it might give her hope.

So anyway, here I sit alone in my room with plenty of studying to do and I'm writing in my diary, feeling slightly sorry for myself. And why is that really? I'm not sure what it is—exactly—but something just doesn't feel right to me.

Josh and I e-mail almost every day. And although I feel closer to him than ever, something just doesn't seem right. And that bugs me. I know we're not doing anything wrong, at least I don't think so, but at the same time I feel uneasy, like I've blown it somehow. I keep asking God to show me and nothing really comes up. And yet I feel sort of unhappy.

I suppose it doesn't help to know that other people are out living and acting like normal college kids. And here I am feeling like a lonely old maid. Now I know that's ridiculous, but it's how I feel. I mean, Lindsey and Kim are out with Stephen and Bryce tonight. I guess I know why Kim was so elated when she learned about Josh and me. It freed up Bryce for her! Not that I really mind. I guess I feel sorta left out. But it's more than that. I have a feeling I've made a big mistake and God's just waiting for me to figure it all out. And I have to admit that makes me feel rather sick inside. But right now I really need to do homework! OH, GOD, PLEASE HELP ME!

Sunday, February 2 (an awakening)

Today's sermon really blew me away. I mean, I've heard the story of Abraham and Isaac before and how God spared Isaac from being sacrificed up there on the mountain. But the way Pastor Obertti told the story today just totally blew my socks off!

He said that God did that whole thing with Abraham and Isaac, first of all, to foreshadow the way God would be willing to sacrifice His own son in order to save the world, but secondly, to teach us all something about our priorities. But let me start at the beginning. You see, God told Abraham that he would be the father of nations, and that his descendents would be more numerous than the stars—which are uncountable, I think. But the problem was he was a really old guy and his wife Sarah was way older than my grandma! So the likelihood of those two senior citizens having dozens of babies was pretty slim. Still, God did the miracle (after

Abraham and Sarah blew it trying to get a baby through Sarah's handmaiden Hagar, but that's another story...).

Anyway, they had the baby Isaac. He was like their promise child—the one God would use to deliver all those uncountable generations through. So obviously Isaac was really, really valuable to them—not to mention beloved since they so badly wanted a child. But can you imagine how poor old Abraham must've felt when God told him to take this precious boy up to the mountain and kill him! Sheesh, there go Abraham's dreams right down the toilet. But this is the amazing thing: Abraham loved God so much and trusted Him so completely that he was actually willing to obey. Still, it had to be tearing him to pieces to think he would actually have to slit his son's throat up on that mountain. Man!

But Pastor Obertti said that we all have our own personal "Isaacs." (Something we love so much that it threatens to overshadow our love for God.) And usually it's not something bad—that would be too obvious. Usually it's something (or someone) that's good and lovable and perhaps even may appear to be a gift from God. He used the example of a woman having a dream to be a missionary, but after a while the dream of foreign missions became more important to her than God, and she had to set it aside to get her priorities straight. He also talked about a man who dearly loved his aging mother—to the point that he wasn't willing to do what

God had called him to do. Then he spoke of a guy who was so distracted by his love for his fiancée that he nearly forgot about God, and he had to get his priorities right.

Okay, you can probably guess where I'm heading with this. I am afraid that Josh may be my "Isaac" and that God is asking me to sacrifice him. Of course I'm not going to kill him, but to be honest (and all lightness aside), it's killing me to consider this. I'm scared that God is telling me to break off this "covenant" with Josh. And if He is telling me to do this, I'm worried that I can't. Because the truth is, I don't want to. I love Josh, and I can imagine spending the rest of my life with him. Oh sure, I may only be eighteen, but I think it's possible to know something like this now. And so I'm feeling really confused. I mean, it seems like God put Josh and me together in the first place. So how can it be that He's breaking us apart now—or wants to?

Of course, I know in the story of Abraham and Isaac that in the last minute, God jumps in (or rather an angel does) and spares Isaac. As a result, Abraham doesn't kill his only son. But this doesn't even happen until Abraham raises the sharpened knife into the air. Arggh! What am I supposed to do with this now?

DEAR GOD, IF YOU'RE REALLY SHOWING ME THIS THING—THAT I NEED TO GIVE UP JOSH IN THE SAME WAY YOU ASKED ABRAHAM TO GIVE UP ISAAC, PLEASE MAKE IT REALLY CRYSTAL CLEAR. OH, I

KNOW YOU WON'T WRITE IT ACROSS THE SKY OR
SHOUT IT FROM THE HEAVENS, BUT PLEASE HELP
ME TO KNOW DEEP DOWN IN MY HEART WHAT IT IS
YOU'RE CALLING ME TO DO. AMEN.

NINETEEN

Thursday, February 6 (what now?)

I've had the most miserable week ever. Not because of classes (although the load is heavy enough) and not because of Liz (who's actually been pretty quiet this week) but because of this whole Isaac/Josh thing. I haven't written a word of this to Josh—I mean, what would I say? As a result, all my communication with him is beginning to feel stilted and phony. But that's not the worst thing.

The worst thing is that I'm starting to feel a barrier rising up between me and God (or maybe it's been there since Christmas and I've only just begun to notice it). Also I have absolutely no peace inside. It's as if a storm is raging—or maybe it's a battle that's waging. I don't even know how to adequately describe it, except to say that it feels miserable. Totally miserable.

And so I know what I must do. And the mere idea of

doing this thing is just killing me inside. But not to do it is a form of torture far worse than death. I feel as if God's asking me to cut off an arm or a leg—or worse. And it scares me to think that I love Josh THAT much—that this would be so painful. I'm thinking: <u>what if</u> he truly IS the great love of my life? And <u>what if</u>, in letting him go, I lose something that I'll never find again—<u>ever?</u> But, on the other hand, <u>what if</u> I hold on to him and permanently lose the TRUE LOVE of my life—God?

Of course, I know what I have to do. What I MUST do. But the question is: Can I? Do I honestly have the strength to let go of Josh? And what about Josh? How is this going to make him feel? Will it crush him, break his heart, wound his spirit? Will we ever be able to be friends again? I mean he's been one of my best friends for the last two years. How did I get into this mess?

OH, GOD, PLEASE HELP ME. I FEEL SO CONFUSED AND UNHAPPY. I NEED YOUR HELP MORE THAN EVER BEFORE.

Friday, February 7

After some more heavy soul-searching, I know, without a doubt, what I must do. I suppose I've known it all along (deep inside). The problem is, I'm just not sure how to do it. The telephone seems like such a weird way to say something as serious as this, plus I'm worried that I'll get all flustered when I hear his voice, and consequently, I won't be able to explain myself clearly. But I hate to e-mail him—that seems like such a cheesy way to communicate something as critical as this. And so I think I'll sit down and write an old-fashioned letter. Not like a "Dear John" hopefully, but something from my heart that will carefully communicate exactly what it is that God is doing in me. I know it's too late to do it tonight, because I need a clear head, but just knowing I've actually made my decision helps some. Oh, I still feel like I'm bleeding inside, but I'm hoping that maybe the pain will go away, maybe in time.

Saturday, February 8 (picking up the knife)

I walked around campus today and thought of how I would write this difficult letter to Josh. And as I rehearsed the words and explanations in my mind, the thought occurred to me that maybe this is all just a test for me. Maybe I'm going to be like Abraham and get clear to the point of raising my knife in the air (or maybe it's my pen) and then God will send an angel to stay my hand, to stop my pen, and to show me that it's okay for me to continue loving Josh. Just as long as I always know that I must love God most and foremost. Maybe that's it.

Sunday, February 9 (the deed is done)

Well, no angel showed up last night. When I sat down to my desk and began writing my letter, absolutely nothing happened to stop me. Liz didn't come home early from her date. The phone never rang. No one knocked on my door. And so I just kept writing and writing and writing. As I wrote, I could see that I was still trying to deceive myself into thinking that this was just a test and that I would only pass this test once I actually dropped the letter into the mailbox. But then—in the midst of writing—a vivid picture came to mind. Okay, not to sound weird, but it was almost like a vision.

Suddenly I imagined or envisioned this thing that was planted in my heart—okay, to be honest, it looked like a weed—like a dandelion. And that dandelion repre-sented Josh. And although I honestly don't see Josh as a weed, I believe that God was showing me he is. Well, I just burst into tears at this thought because I totally love Josh. I really do! How could he possibly be a weed of all things? He is a good and decent person—and he loves God with his whole heart. I believe this. But then it slowly became clearer, kind of like the clouds parting, that it was only for me that Josh is a weed. And I felt that God was showing me that as I obeyed and wrote that letter, I was pulling the weed from my heart.

And so I thought, well, okay, if that's really what God wants me to do, I can do it. I mean, it might be hard and feel painful, but I can do it. Still, as I'm writing the letter, I'm crying so much that the tears keep messing up the pages. But I keep on writing, just pouring out my heart to Josh.

But then as I finish writing and feel that at last I'm

done, it hits me that although I may have pulled off the top part of the weed (by writing the letter), the roots of the weed (the hope that this all is just a test) are still planted deeply in my heart, and somehow I know that God wants me to take a trowel or something equally sharp and dig the roots out.

So now I'm really sobbing, wondering how it is that a loving God could ask me to endure such seemingly senseless and endless pain? And why is He saying that Josh is like a weed? Am I just imagining this whole thing? (Although I know I'm not.) And I don't know how I can possibly continue digging into my heart to remove all those tiny little roots—memories of all the good as well as bad times that Josh and I have shared over the past couple years? How can a mere human being do such a hard thing?

But just as I felt I might give up, that this task was too much for me, I suddenly felt a strong and comforting assurance that I only needed to yield my heart to God (the Gardener), and if I let Him, He would do the work for me. And so that's what I did (and what I am doing). Still, I can't say that it's easy or that I feel especially good, because the truth is, I feel somewhat numb right now. However, I did drop the letter in the mailbox today (even though it's Sunday) because I didn't trust myself to hang on to it until tomorrow. I was afraid I might've thrown it away.

And to be honest, I feel emotionally spent and drained—like I could just sleep for a week. But despite

this, I also feel a very real sense of peace that is inde-
scribable. And I'm thinking that I did, after all, really do
the right thing. That is a comfort.

Monday, February 10 (glimmer of hope)

Today, for the first time in weeks, I actually experienced
a real sense of joy. Okay, it wasn't a jumping-up-and-down,
I'm-so-excited kind of joy. But it was real just the same. I
feel certain it's from God. And the truth is, I haven't
felt that deep sense of joy since before Christmas,
before I made that covenant commitment to Josh. And so
I'm feeling more certain than ever that it really was
God showing me that my decision was wrong.

Even so, I've been fighting off some anxiety in
regards to Josh's reaction to my letter. I know he won't
get it until tomorrow or maybe even Wednesday. And I
have no idea what he'll do or think or how he'll respond.
Every time I think about this whole ugly business, I get
this awful knot in the pit of my stomach, and I honestly
think I could just toss my cookies.

But then I pray that God will strengthen me as well
as help Josh to understand this whole thing. And I'm
thinking: If this relationship is wrong for me, then it has
to be wrong for Josh too. Isn't that obvious? So I just
hope he can see this too. And maybe he'll even be
thankful; maybe we can still be friends. And although
I know I must keep giving the whole thing up (to get rid
of all those roots), I still fight against this faint hope

that in due time (God's time, of course) He will restore our relationship—better than ever. But you never know; He may not. And I know I have to be able to accept this possibility—joyfully. The amazing thing is I almost think I can.

Wednesday, February 12 (the wait)

Still no word from Josh. Thankfully I didn't even get an e-mail from him today. I responded to the one from him yesterday with a quick note saying I couldn't talk just then, but that he should watch for my letter. I've been praying for him off and on all day. I absolutely hate the idea of me hurting him in any way. And it makes me realize how wrong it was for me to accept that ring in the first place. I mean, it was a serious commitment that I entered into way too lightly. Even at the time I said "yes," I know I didn't have perfect peace in my heart. I realize that now with twenty-twenty hindsight, but I should've known it was God's way of checking me then. Unfortunately I was uncheckable. And that bothers me a lot.

The one good thing is that it makes me want to press into God more than ever before. I don't ever want to be that spiritually dense again. Never! I realize I was probably just caught up in the moment, swept away by the fun and glamour and what have you...but really, is that any kind of excuse? And although I realize God forgives me, and I'm ever so thankful for that, I also feel that I need

Josh to forgive me as well. And, yes, I need to forgive myself.

Despite these worrisome feelings, I still have a deep sense of peace. I totally <u>know</u> without a shadow of doubt that I did the right thing. But it's a peace mixed with sadness—or maybe it's remorse—that I allowed myself (and poor Josh) to get into this situation to start with. Oh, it's so much easier to avoid mistakes in the first place than to clean them up afterward. Hearts and feelings are not easily mended, I fear.

Thursday, February 13

Ironically, tomorrow is Valentine's Day—the big day to celebrate romance and true love. It's as if this day has arrived just in time to mock me—to make me feel regret or stupidity or anger. But I refuse to give in to it. I know (despite my tumultuous feelings) that I AM obeying God. And even though it's not always "fun" to obey, it's still right and good and, in the end, very, very worthwhile. So I am just tuning out the hearts and cupids and chocolates and flowers. My heart belongs to God.

And as fate (or God) would have it, I still haven't heard a single word from Josh. I suppose it's possible he hasn't received my letter or perhaps hasn't had time to read it. However, I don't think that's likely. And since he has noticeably NOT e-mailed me, I'm afraid he's gotten the letter and is just too plain angry or hurt or maybe both to speak to me. Oh, I feel so bad about this whole thing. I just want it to be over. And, yes, I wish—oh, man, how I wish that I'd never, ever said that fateful "yes."

PLEASE, GOD, HELP ME TO NEVER MAKE A BLUNDER LIKE THIS AGAIN. AND, PLEASE, PLEASE, HELP JOSH TO SEE YOUR WILL IN ALL THIS. I KNOW JOSH LOVES YOU AND WANTS TO SERVE YOU. I KNOW HE'LL UNDERSTAND—IF NOT IMMEDIATELY—IN DUE TIME. ONCE AGAIN, GOD, I'M SORRY. I'M SO SORRY. AMEN.

Friday, February 14 (Happy Valentine's Day)

I think this day will go down on record as the most horrible, detestable, unforgettable, despicable, unendurable, torturous Valentine's Day ever (at least for me, that is). I'm sure some people are having a good time. Like Liz, for instance. She has a box of chocolates and a single red rose sitting on her desk right now. And Kim told me that despite Lindsey's "too young" speech, she and Stephen are now talking about getting engaged. And I suspect that Kim is head over heels for Bryce these days, although she hasn't admitted as much. It's like the whole world is in love!

To make matters worse, I hadn't wanted to tell anyone about breaking up with Josh—not until I heard back from him, that is. Which I haven't. And it's driving me nuts! I can't stand it. I feel like I'm going to burst if he doesn't call or e-mail or respond somehow—and soon.

Liz walked into our room this afternoon to find me pacing and literally wringing my hands. And despite my promise to myself (to remain silent until I hear from Josh), I sat down and tearfully poured out the whole embarrassing story to her. And, honestly, as soon as it was done I felt totally lame—like maybe I was "casting my pearls before swine" since she's obviously not a believer and I had just stupidly shared the most intimate contents of my heart—giving her an open invitation to stomp all over them. But the cool thing is, <u>she didn't.</u> To my stunned amazement, she turned out to be a really understanding listener. And she never gloated or said "I told you so"—which she could've since she had, from the beginning, thought it was a dumb idea.

"Well, I know we don't believe in the same things," she began in what seemed a careful manner, especially for Liz, "but somehow what you're saying actually makes sense to me. And for what it's worth, I think you did the right thing."

"Really?" I wiped my nose and stared at her curiously. The fact that Liz thought I'd done the right thing could be both comforting and frightening at the same time. And at that moment, I wasn't quite sure how to feel.

"Do <u>you</u> think you did the right thing?"

I sniffed. "Actually, I really do. I mean, once I'd mailed that letter, I felt a real sense of peace return to my heart."

She nodded. "As a casual observer, I have to admit that you didn't seem quite yourself after Christmas break. I suppose we've both changing, and maybe I'm seeing things somewhat differently, but you just seemed—well, sort of unhappy, I guess."

"You could actually see that?"

She nodded. "Something in your eyes was different."

"Wow. That's amazing."

She laughed. "I may not be a Christian, but I'm not blind either."

We talked a little bit more, and then she left to meet Conrad for their special Valentine's date. And I've been sitting by the phone, trying to study, but more distracted than ever. It's so weird to think of Josh having received that letter by now, having read it, possibly reacting to it, and yet saying nothing to me. And on top of that, here it is Valentine's Day! I almost wonder if he might be trying to punish me. Should I e-mail him? Call him? What? Or do I wait for him? I don't know what to do, but I'm praying that God will show me. Soon!

Saturday, February 15

Josh made a startling appearance on campus today. I could've actually fainted when Liz opened the door and I heard his voice speaking as plain as day.

"Hi, I'm Josh Miller," he said politely. "Is this Caitlin O'Conner's room?"

Fortunately, he couldn't see me because of the door, and it took me a few seconds to compose myself and find my voice.

"Josh?" I stepped out and tried to smile, although I'm sure it looked foolish and my knees felt like noodles. "What are you—?"

"We need to talk, Caitlin." His expression was hard and cold and very unJoshlike.

"Yeah, okay. Let me get my coat." I grabbed my coat, also picking up the little blue velvet box that had been sitting on my desk for the last week. I slipped it into my pocket and joined him in the hallway, not failing to notice Liz giving me a nod of encouragement as I exited the room.

Soon we were outside, walking silently in the cold evening air. I wasn't sure if I could even speak intelligibly, and my stomach felt as if it had risen to my throat, but somehow I suggested we duck into the coffee shop, or maybe it was his idea. Anyway we got there, somehow.

"You...uh...you got my letter," I stammered once we were seated with steaming mugs of coffee before us. Of course, it was obvious he'd gotten my letter. But what was I supposed to say? I felt totally disoriented, like a fish out of water. To be perfectly honest, at this awkward point, I even wondered if he wasn't here to try to talk me out of this whole breaking up thing.

Embarrassingly enough, I think I almost hoped he was! I almost hoped I'd say something like: "Oh, that letter was all just a silly mistake, Josh. I'm so sorry; I guess I must've gotten cold feet. I never should've written it." And it scares me to the depths of my soul to think I actually thought those very words, but that is the honest-to-God truth! And He knows it.

"That was some letter." He pressed his lips together then took a slow sip of coffee.

I took a deep breath. "Did you understand what I was saying?"

"I'm not stupid, Caitlin. You made everything perfectly clear."

"And you're...uh...okay?"

He shrugged. "What am I going to do?"

I looked down at the overhead lights reflecting on the surface of my coffee. Suddenly it felt as if a heavy weight was pressing down on my chest, almost as if I couldn't breathe. I knew I had to say something. "I'm sorry if I hurt you—"

"Don't be."

"But, Josh—"

"Caitlin, you did what you thought God told you to do, right?"

I looked up at him. His eyes still had that strange, hardened look. "Yes, but—"

"No buts. If you did what God told you to do, who am I to argue?"

"I don't want to argue. I just want to talk—"

"There's nothing more to say."

"Then why did you come here?"

He looked at me, and it seemed as if his blue eyes were softening, just a little. "I wanted to see you face-to-face—just to see."

"To see?"

He exhaled loudly then set down his mug with a loud thump. "Oh, I don't know. I guess I hoped I'd see something—I don't know what."

I reached for his hand, but he moved it. "Josh, I'm really sorry."

"You said that already."

"But this just feels all wrong."

He laughed but not a happy laugh. "And you expect it to feel—what? All right? Good and nice and happy?"

"No, but, not—not like this."

He started to stand now. "I really don't have anything else to say."

"But—"

"I'm going to see if I can spend the night with Stephen tonight." He pushed the stool back in and squared his shoulders, but I could see his eyes glistening with tears. "You need me to walk you back?"

I shook my head, trying to swallow back my own tears. Then I remembered the ring. I pulled the box out of my pocket. "Here."

He shoved his hands in his pockets. "Just keep it."

"But I don't want—"

"Look, I certainly don't want it. I don't care what you do with it. Okay?" And then he turned and left.

I stayed in the coffee shop a little longer, too stunned to leave. And it felt as if my heart were splitting in two, right then. I mean, it physically felt like it was tearing apart. And as excruciatingly painful as that felt, I still could sense that quiet reassuring peace within me.

It's hard to describe how you can feel peace and pain like that, simultaneously, but somehow I did.

I prayed with each step as I walked back to the dorm. I prayed that God would help Josh through this whole thing and that somehow He would strengthen Josh because of it. And I prayed the same thing for me.

Liz was gone when I returned, but there was a little chocolate kiss on my desk with a Post-it note that said, "sorry." I knew it was her way to make me feel better, but I burst into tears just the same.

I cried for a long, long time. Why? Not because I was losing Josh. No, I knew I'd already lost him—back when I mailed that letter. No, I cried because I realized my own responsibility in this whole thing. It was largely my fault that Josh was hurting so badly right now. Sure, he may have been the one to bring the whole covenant thing up to me. But I was the one who said yes. Oh, if only I'd said no. Maybe we could've just discussed the whole thing openly right then, and maybe we'd still be friends now. I'm afraid we'll never be friends again. I think that's part of what hurts so much tonight.

And yet God's peace remains. Without that I'm sure I'd have died from the pain.

DEAR GOD, I FEEL LIKE I'VE AGED A HUNDRED YEARS TONIGHT. I GUESS PAIN IS LIKE THAT. PLEASE HELP JOSH TO GROW STRONGER AS A RESULT OF THIS. AND IF IT'S EVER POSSIBLE TO

RESTORE OUR FRIENDSHIP, I PRAY THAT YOU WILL. IN THE MEANTIME, I TRUST YOU WITH EVERY- THING. AND, ONCE AGAIN, I'M SORRY. AMEN.

TWENTY

Friday, March 14 *(moving on)*

Next week is finals week, and to say
I'm relieved would be a huge understatement. This has
been a hard term in several ways. But I suppose having
an overload of classes was something of a relief in itself.
Being so busy gave me less time to fret over the way
things went with my breakup with Josh. I haven't seen or
spoken to him since that chilly night in February almost a
month ago. Although I have heard (through Chloe) that
he's kept himself busy with school too. And (she thinks)
he's still pretty bummed by the whole thing.

"Josh is used to always having things go his way," she
explained during her unexpected visit last weekend.
(She'd hopped on a bus just to come cheer me up.) "And
I'm sure he still hasn't gotten over the shock of being
rejected."

"I didn't exactly reject <u>him</u>, not personally anyway," I said, knowing it made little sense. "I mostly rejected the idea of being tied to him after God corrected me about the whole thing. I knew it was wrong to stay with Josh when I realized our relationship was taking priority over my relationship with God. I still think Josh is a really great guy."

"Oh, I know that. But maybe God is using this whole thing to teach him something important."

I smiled. It still strikes me as funny, or maybe just ironic, to hear such words of wisdom spouting from this fifteen-year-old mouth. But then that's Chloe.

Liz actually got a kick out of my young friend. (She couldn't believe she was the little sister of "that preppy Josh" as Liz still calls him after only one brief encounter—although she did admit he was "rather nice looking.") Anyway, Liz didn't even mind the extra roommate bunking on our floor that Saturday night.

"Do you know what Josh plans to do on spring break?" I asked casually as I walked Chloe to the bus station on Sunday. To be honest, I was hoping he wasn't planning on going home. I didn't want to chance an uncomfortable encounter with him at church or wherever.

"Didn't you know?"

"What?"

"He's going down to Mexico."

"You're kidding? To the mission?"

She nodded and readjusted her backpack.

"Well, that's cool." But even as I said the words, I felt a tiny wave of jealousy ripple over me. Suddenly I wished

I could go too. Not to be with him exactly, but just to be down there to help with the kids.

"Yeah, it was kind of spur-of-the-moment. But they'd raised some money at his college. It's for some new building the mission has been wanting, and Josh decided to hand deliver it and help out."

"That's great. Our fellowship group's talking about a fund-raiser, but we haven't really gotten it off the ground yet."

"Well, my parents weren't overly thrilled about Josh's unexpected trip." She chuckled. "They'd been talking about having us all take a little Caribbean cruise together."

"Oh, that's too bad."

"Not for me." She made a face. "I won't mind missing out on that little boat ride. Besides..." She grinned suspiciously.

"What?"

"Well, I haven't even told my folks about this yet. But remember I mentioned how these two girls and I have been jamming together lately—just for fun?"

"Yeah—isn't that Allie and Laura?"

"Right. Well, we've got ourselves an actual gig that same week. Remember that Christian coffeehouse you took me to last year?"

"Yeah. You're going to play there?"

"Yep. On Friday night. Hey, do you think you can come?"

"You bet. I wouldn't miss it. Maybe Beanie and Jenny

will want to come too. They plan to be around during spring break."

"Cool. We could use some enthusiastic fans."

By then we were at the bus station, and her bus was already loading up. "Thanks for coming to see me, Chloe." I gave her a big hug. "It really meant a lot to me."

"Well, you seemed pretty down." She smiled. "And I suppose I was still feeling a little bummed to think you'll probably never be my sister-in-law now."

I remembered the letdown I'd given her just the night before when she asked if there might be a slight possibility that Josh and I would eventually get married someday. "But I can still be like your sister."

"Yeah, that works." Then she climbed on the bus and waved.

I suppose my words may have been a little strong that night, but I hadn't wanted to give her any false hopes. I wanted her to understand, more than anything, that I just want to obey God, and I believe He's closed the door with Josh. But I assured Chloe that I still love Josh as a friend and brother, and although I feel sorry he and I can't still be friends, I want, more than anything else, to remain obedient to God.

For all I know, God might want me to be single for the rest of my days. And I told Chloe how I need to be willing to accept that. I actually think she understood. As I've said, Chloe seems wise beyond her years.

Tuesday, March 25 (signs of spring)

Finals seemed to go okay last week (at least I hope so!). I caught a ride home with Bryce last weekend and have been enjoying just hanging with family and friends the past couple of days. It's weird though; everyone is still acting all apologetic and sorry to me about my breakup with Josh. Well, not everyone. Beanie definitely thinks it was a smart move. And I suppose my dad's relieved. And Tony too. But the others act like it's something to be sad about. And the truth is, I'm tired of explaining it over and over, so I just accept their sympathy and hope they'll move on. I know I have.

It's like this deep down joy has been growing in me—ever since that dark day when Josh came to visit. It's hard to explain, but I think it's kind of like springtime. It's that feeling that life and growth are just beginning to bud after a long, cold winter. I feel like those tulips and daffodils, with their cheery, hopeful faces looking up to the sun, as if life is just beginning! There is nothing on earth as satisfying as walking with God—in perfect obedience. Okay, I know I'm not perfect, but I really am trying to do what God wants me to do. And I think His reward is that sweet, pure joy and peace. And it's a good thing!

Friday, March 28

Beanie, Jenny, Anna, and I went to hear Chloe and her friends perform last night at the Christian coffeehouse.

And, believe me, we were all totally blown away by this young trio. In fact, everyone there was impressed. These high school girls are really good! Despite not wanting to run into him, I wish Josh could've been there to see his little sister perform. It was amazing. The girls' voices blended perfectly, and every song was an original that Chloe had penned herself. I'm thinking that girl may be a genius! A number of people asked if they were selling CDs afterward, and Chloe said she plans to discuss the possibility of getting one recorded with her dad's friend (the music teacher from the college). But honestly, I think these girls could be a big hit! I can't even describe how proud I am of Chloe. I know it doesn't really have anything to do with me, but I can't help but feel a certain type of motherly—or maybe sisterly—pride in Chloe's success.

Sunday, April 6

This has been a totally great week for me. It's the first week of spring term, and I've got a manageable class schedule, plus time to attend the fellowship group and to just hang with friends. If anyone had told me I'd be this happy six months ago (back when I just started school and was feeling completely homesick and depressed), I never would've believed her. But the truth is, I was really happy to get back to school this term. And I was glad to see Liz again. Our friendship has really grown in the past several months. Oh sure, we're not <u>best</u> friends, and she can still be a pain in the behind sometimes when she's in one of her foul moods, and, yes, she's still not a Christian, but I really do love her—and I think it's just a matter of time before she returns to God (although I wouldn't admit this to her).

Another great thing that's happening—our fellowship group has started working toward a fund-raiser for Mexico. We're going to put on a really fancy dinner at the church (a hundred dollars a plate!) followed by a silent auction. I've already started hitting businesses for donations, and when I went to the campus gift shop (where I'd gotten Liz that little lamb for last Christmas), the woman asked me if I was looking for any part-time work. Well, I hadn't actually been looking, but it suddenly occurred to me that it might not be a bad idea after all. And anyway, I start working next week. Just a couple evenings a week and on Saturdays, but since I have a lighter class load this term, plus I'm looking to earn money to go to Mexico this summer—well, it all seemed just perfect. A God thing!

After church today, a bunch of us took a bike ride. And it was so great! The weather was absolutely perfect and spring was busting out all over! And as I was sailing down a hill with the wind in my face, it hit me— I felt so free! And suddenly I wondered how I would've felt if I were still tied into that commitment with Josh. And in that instant I realized, with crystal-clear clarity, that I was exactly where God wanted me to be. How great is that?

Saturday, April 12 (an unexpected visit)

I was awakened early this morning by the phone's shrill ring. I groggily picked it up and croaked out a froglike "hello" only to hear what sounded just like Josh on the other end! Blown away by this possibility, I decided I must've been dreaming and almost hung up. But he said "hello" again, and I realized it must be for real. A wave of shock ran through me as I sat up in bed, blinking to clear my eyes and fuzzy brain.

"Caitlin?" he spoke quietly, in what seemed a tentative voice, especially for the usually self-assured Josh Miller. "Is that you?"

"Josh?"

"Yeah," another pause. "I was in town, and I...uh...I wondered if I could meet you—"

"You're kidding? You're here on campus? Right now?"

"Yeah. I drove over last night."

Suddenly, I felt seriously worried. Was he here to pressure me into going back with him? Or was he still angry with me? What was up?

"So...uh...can we get together, Caitlin?"

"I..." I ran my fingers through my hair wondering what I should do, then shot up a quick prayer. Finally, sensing no harm could come from simply talking with him, I agreed to meet him at the coffee shop in half an hour.

I quickly showered and dressed, praying all the while that God would quiet my heart and lead me through what promised to be a difficult meeting. Then I hurried over to the coffee shop to find Josh already seated and sipping coffee.

"Hi." I ordered a large double mocha and then joined him. "What's up?"

"Sorry to catch you by surprise," he began. And as I looked at him, I sensed something was different, but I couldn't quite put my finger on it.

"It's okay. I probably needed to get up anyway." I paused as the waiter set my cup before me. "So what are you doing over here, Josh?"

He looked at me evenly. "I came to apologize to you, Caitlin. I need to ask you to forgive me."

"Forgive you?"

He nodded. "Yeah. I realize now that I never should've asked you to join in that covenant thing with me."

"You're kidding?" Now to be honest, I was having a confusing mix of thoughts just then. Was Josh saying that it had been a mistake because he never really wanted to marry me in the first place (and right or wrong, this thought hurt my ego more than a little), or was he just saying that it was wrong?

He shook his head. "No, I can see now that it wasn't God leading me—it was something that I had devised myself." He looked down at the table. "I suppose I tried to make myself believe it was God, at the time—because I wanted it so much."

"Oh, Josh." I controlled my hand from reaching out to touch him.

"But I can see now that not only was it stupid, but it was dangerous too."

"Dangerous?"

"Yeah, it's that kind of thinking that leads people right into legalism and even a cult type of mentality."

"Really?" I had never considered this possibility before.

"But the worst part of the whole thing was that I involved you—I put you in a really bad position."

"But it was my own fault for agreeing—"

"You never would've agreed if I hadn't brought it up and then pressured you." He looked me straight in the eyes. "I'm sorry, Caitlin. Will you please forgive me?"

"Oh, Josh, of course, I forgive you. I already did forgive you." I smiled. "How could I not?"

His countenance lightened a little. "Yeah, I should have known that you would've already done the right thing. That's just the way you are."

I sighed. "Well, I don't know about that. To be honest, I was hurt and upset at you for a while, but mostly I felt like it was my own fault—I never should've agreed to do something I knew in my heart was wrong." Then I looked at him. "Can you forgive me, Josh?"

He smiled. "Sure. But I still think it was mostly my fault."

"Well, let's not argue about that." I took a sip of coffee. "Tell me how you've been? How was your trip to Mexico?"

"Really great. It was kind of a spur-of-the-moment

decision, but I'm glad I went. I think I needed it—probably even more than they needed me."

"I heard you guys raised enough money for the new preschool."

"Yeah, it was amazing! The folks down there were so surprised and happy. It was pretty cool."

I nodded. "Well, I have to admit I was a little envious when I heard that you were going down there. I wished I could've gone too."

"Really? You should've come."

I laughed. "Yeah, after all we've been through—you really think that would've been a good idea?"

"Maybe not."

"But I'm planning on going this summer. I've got a part-time job, and I've already started saving up for it. I'd like to stay for a whole month or maybe even more if I can."

"Really? I was thinking of doing something along the same lines. I'd really like to help them with some of the building projects that are coming up."

Suddenly I felt a little unsure. "Uh, do you think it'd be a problem for...uh...for us, I mean, if we happened to be there at the same time?"

He shrugged. "I don't see why it should be a problem. In fact, I was hoping that we could go back to being good friends again, Caitlin. I miss you."

I smiled. "I miss you too. But do you think it's possible to be just friends?"

"You mean do I think I can control myself and keep

from coming on to you or pressuring you into marrying me or something equally crazy?"

I laughed. "Well, something like that."

He held up his hand as if to make a pledge. "I give you my scout's honor that I'll do my very best to keep our relationship as that of good friends—brother and sister. Does that suit you okay?"

I nodded. "Yeah. That suits me just fine."

"Can I ask you something?"

"Sure."

"Well, you know what you said in the letter about me being a weed that God had to pull from your heart?"

I winced. "Yeah?"

"Do you really think of me like that?"

"Oh, Josh." I made a face. "Not at all. But it's like you'd taken root in my heart—rather I'd allowed you to take root—and it wasn't God's plan for me right now. And it was important for my relationship with God that I remove you."

"And have you?"

I took a deep breath. "I believe I have."

"But you said 'right now.' Does that mean things could change later on?"

I smiled. "I don't know. I guess it's up to God."

He nodded. "Yeah, I can see that."

"You must know that I still love you, Josh. You've been one of my best friends. You've been like a brother."

"But that's all."

"That's all for right now."

"There's that phrase again. Right now."

I ran my fingers over the warm cup. "Well, you know, we can only live one day at time. Who knows what the future might bring? But for now, yes, that's all."

He smiled. "Okay, that works for me."

Then he showed me some snapshots he'd taken in Mexico. And we talked and laughed some more. And when it was all said and done, I felt as though our friendship was probably more secure than ever before. It's like we'd weathered the storm and come out stronger for it. And only God knows what lies ahead for us. I can trust Him with that.

"I'm so glad you came," I told Josh as he walked me back to the dorm.

"Me too." He squinted up at the morning sun. "I didn't want to, but I knew God was telling me to clean this whole mess that I'd made up."

"Well, at least we can learn from our messes. Right?"

"Yeah. Hopefully I'll learn not to keep repeating them."

I stopped by the steps in front of my dorm and really looked at him. "I think you've changed, Josh."

He frowned slightly. "Like how?"

"I mean for the better." I studied him. "It's as if your spirit seems softer or more humble or something. I'm not exactly sure, but for some reason you seem..." I struggled for the right words. "More like Jesus."

Now his old smile came back, only this time there was more depth to it. "Thanks, Cate. There's nothing you could've said that means more to me than that."

I could feel tears glistening in my eyes just then, but they were happy tears. "Is it okay if I hug you—just as a friend, I mean?"

Then we hugged—like friends—and I told him I loved him. "Like a brother," I said as I stepped back.

"You take care, Sis!" he called as he headed for his Jeep. "And don't forget to stay in touch!"

"Don't worry." I waved. "You know how I love to write."

TWENTY-ONE

Saturday, April 26
(sigh of relief)

I spent the day alone with God today, and it
was totally great! First I rode my bike to a park on the
other side of town, and then I sat by the river and just
read my Bible and prayed and meditated on how amazingly gracious God has been to me. I think it's good to
take times like this (I should probably do it a whole lot
more!) to get a better perspective of who God is and
what He's doing in your life. But when you do, you should
always be prepared to be amazed! Because God is like
that. He totally blows me away with His love and His
mercy and His grace. I can't even wrap my mind around
it. And yet it's good to try.

My first year away from home has certainly had its
ups and downs, but now I can clearly see God's hand in it.
And I'm totally thankful for the way things have gone. I
remember how I was all upset when I first realized I had

to go to the state university. But now I can see that it was the right thing for me. I've made some really great Christian friends, and my relationship with Liz is better than ever. I wouldn't be surprised if she doesn't actually come to church with me tomorrow—she's mentioned that she wants to "give it a try" before the end of the term.

And then there was that whole thing with Josh. Even though it was painful, it was probably one of the best lessons on obeying God that I've ever had to learn. I can see now that nothing is more important for me than to know how to hear God and to obey—quickly!

So, here I am, with almost a whole year of college under my belt, on my own, and feeling really good about life. And you know what? I feel as though I could follow God anywhere now. Whether it's Mexico or Somalia or Nepal or my own hometown...I'm totally willing to go wherever God leads me. I feel like I don't need my parents anymore—I mean, not like I used to need them. I suppose I'll always need them in some ways. And I don't need my old best friends (Beanie, Jenny, and Anna) always constantly by my side—although I still love them dearly. And I don't even need Josh to lean on—but I'm glad he's my friend. And like I said, who knows what God has in store for us. But the thing is: I finally understand that I will really and truly be just fine on my own—as long as God is with me. Because with God, even when I'm on my own, I am never really alone. I can always count on Him. No matter what else happens in my life, He will always be with me, He will never leave me or forsake me or betray

me—ever. <u>He will always be my best friend—forever!</u>
A poem I wrote on the riverbank:

I'll never be lonely
Even if I am alone
For I've a precious Savior
Who'll come take me home.
But while I'm here
His servant I will be
With one foot on earth
And one in eternity.
And I'll gather His crops
To populate His land
And if I feel weary
I'll cling tighter to His hand.

Multnomah Publishers

The publisher and author would love to hear your
comments about this book. *Please contact us at:*
www.multnomah.net/diary

a personal note from Caitlin...

Dear Friend,

Do you feel like God is nudging at your heart to make a commitment to Him—any sort of commitment? It's best not to put it off, you know. Hey, remember what happened to me???

So...I invite you to sit down right now before God and consider how He may be leading you. Is He asking you to give Him your heart today? Is He asking you to dedicate your body to Him first and abstain from sex until after marriage? Can you hear His voice speaking to you?

Sometimes it helps to write this kind of promise down. You can do that in your diary like I did, or you can write it down here. Then hide it away if you like, but just don't forget it. Because a promise like this is important—both to you and to God. Because you're His child, and He's always listening.

Blessings!

Caitlin O' Conner

❧ *My Promise to God* ❧

I, _____, make a vow to God

Print Name Here

on this day _____ that my heart belongs to Him.

Print Date Here

And I make a vow to God, with His help, to abstain from sex

until I marry.

_____

Your Signature

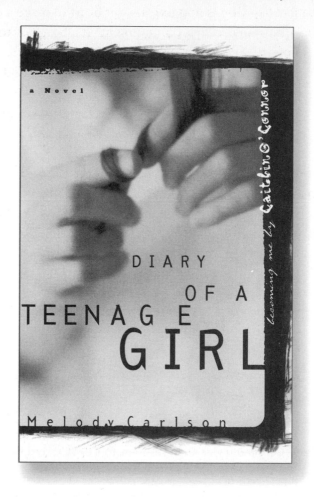

Follow Caitlin O'Conner, a girl much like yourself...

As she makes her way from New Year's to the first day of summer—surviving a challenging home life, changing friends, school pressures, an identity crisis, and the uncertanties of "true love." You'll cry with Caitlin as she experiences heartache, and cheer for her as she encounters a new reality in her life: God. See how rejection by one group can—incredibly—sometimes lead you to discover who you really are...

ISBN 1-57673-735-7

DIARY OF A TEENAGE GIRL SERIES, BOOK 2

Caitlin's Story Continues: Her Commitment to Christ Tested by Time...

Caitlin O'Conner faces new trials as she grows in her faith and strives to maintain the recent commitments she's made to God. As a new believer, Caitlin begins her summer job and makes preparations for a Mexico mission trip with her church youth group. Torn between new spiritual directions and loyalty to Beanie, her best friend, Caitlin searches out her personal values on friendship, romance, dating, life goals, and key relationships with God and family. Her year climaxes in the realization that maturity sometimes means life-impacting decisions must be made... by faith alone.

ISBN 1-59052-053-X

DIARY OF A TEENAGE GIRL SERIES, BOOK 3

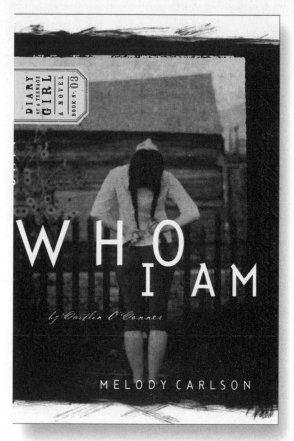

Caitlin's Search for Spirituality, Truth, and Meaning Continues...

It's challenging enough to be a normal high school senior—but Caitlin O'Conner has a host of new difficulties to deal with in the third book of Melody Carlson's widely popular and fascinating teen series. Time is critical to help the orphans in Mexico, missions-minded Caitlin believes, but Mom and Dad are set on her attending college. Meanwhile, her relationship with Josh takes on a serious tone via e-mail—threatening her commitment to "kiss dating goodbye." When Beanie begins dating an African-American, Caitlin's concern over dating seems to be misread as racism. One thing is obvious: God is at work through this dynamic girl in very real but puzzling ways. A soul-stretching time of racial reconciliation at school and within her church helps her discover God's will as never before.

ISBN 1-57673-890-6

HEY, GOD, WHAT DO YOU WANT FROM ME?

More and more teens find themselves growing up in a world lacking in godly wisdom and direction. In *Piercing Proverbs,* bestselling youth fiction author Melody Carlson offers solid messages of the Bible in a version that can compete with TV, movies, and the Internet for the attention of this vital group in God's kingdom. Choosing life-impacting portions of teen-applicable Proverbs, Carlson paraphrases them into understandable, teen-friendly language and presents them as guidelines for clearly identified areas of life (such as friendship, family, money, and mistakes). Teens will easily read and digest these high-impact passages of the Bible delivered in their own words.

ISBN 1-57673-895-7